STAR DEFENDERS

MY ALIEN MATES BOOK 2

MAGGIE ALABASTER

"THE IF HAS CONCLUDED—" J'avet's eyes scanned the room. His gaze settled on me and the sides of his mouth drew back. He looked away before I could flick him the finger.

He continued as though he hadn't paused. "The attack on the *Infinity* intended to slow the ship. The explosives were intended to incite panic, not destruction."

"It would have been good to know that before we evacuated," I muttered.

Beside me, Slek murmured his agreement and his hand tightened in mine. As a ship's engineer, he hadn't been called upon to assess the damage before we piled into pods and fled. His admittedly large ego survived that slightly, but the encounter with the Iri and their nanobot symbionts who had tried to inhabit him and Danec, could have ended badly for us all, especially them.

"However," J'avet continued, "the perpetrator, or perpetrators, remain unknown and at large. We suspect they were a member of a group of rogue Freytaurians, but that's all we know. Consider everyone on *Infinity* at that time to be a suspect."

I expected him to look at me and the Freytaurians who sat to either side of me, but he didn't.

Evidently, Danec expected the same, because he exhaled loudly out his nose when J'avet turned away.

"Commander." Slek stuck his arm up in the air like a schoolboy. "I assume I'm exempt from suspicion, because I was, you know, pushed."

J'avet turned around slowly. "That was only speculation, Engineer. We have proof of nothing."

Slek lowered his hand, and his expression went with it.

I patted his knee. "We know you did nothing wrong," I said loud enough for J'avet to hear.

Typically, the Parvoran ignored me. That was probably just as well. I was done listening to him and I might be tempted to tell him that. While technically he wasn't in charge of me, he could make my life difficult if he wanted to.

"Those of you still going to Agus, the *Halcyon* leaves Dendra Station in two days' time, at fifteen hundred hours precisely." J'avet's eyes swept over the room and settled on me again.

"I'll be on time," I said sweetly.

Before I even finished my sentence, his gaze moved to Danec, and then to someone behind us.

Asshole.

"Dismissed," J'avet said finally. He strode out of the room, full of his own importance, leaving the rest of us to file out of the debriefing in small, quiet groups.

"Someone went to a lot of trouble to keep *Infinity* from protecting the Iri," Brinley said. My friend, and the best pilot in the galaxy—okay, I'm biased, but she is amazing at her job—frowned. Not even a scowl could mar her pretty features. She flicked her hair over her shoulder. "And *Artemis*."

Of the two, we fared better. The *Artemis* was completely destroyed.

"What if it wasn't the rogues which attacked *Infinity*?" Danec asked softly.

"What do you mean?" I asked.

He shrugged. "I-I don't know. Maybe someone wanted us to go to Calig." Colour crept up his already blue face.

"Like an Iri spy, sent to force us to go there to become nanobot hosts?" Slek asked.

"S-something like that," Danec stammered slightly, as he did when nervous or anxious.

"That would mean there's someone ready to throw every Freytaurian to the nanobots." I shivered. "Who would do that?"

"I don't know," Danec said. "Someone who doesn't like Freytaurians?"

"How could anyone not like us?" Slek asked. As a Freytaurian himself, his skin tended toward purple, rather than blue, and he was more street smart than Danec, but they both shared the same vulnerability to the nanobots.

"I can't think of a single reason," I said lightly. "But this would cast suspicion on everyone on board the *Infinity*." I hated to agree with J'avet, but he was right about that.

I stopped beside a window which looked out over Dendra Station. *Infinity* floated beside a dock she shared with a dozen other ships of various sizes. From this angle, she looked whole, undamaged. I knew she was crawling with engineers who worked quickly to fix the IF vessel and press her back into service. I also knew Slek itched to be one of them. He requested to help, but that was denied. It seemed the IF wasn't allowing any passengers from her last voyage to board for any reason. I took that to mean they still searched for tampering or explosives. They wouldn't want us to remove evidence which might implicate us.

Surely since the IF was letting us leave Dendra, they had determined our innocence? That, or they hadn't found proof of guilt. Nor would they. I wouldn't even know how to tamper with a spaceship if I wanted to. Which I didn't. I was a nurse. Of the four of us, Slek and perhaps Brinley were the only ones with that kind of knowledge.

"So, two more nights here, hmmm?" Slek said. He slung an arm over my shoulder and toyed with my hair. He was fascinated with my crazy curls. I was fascinated with his ridiculously enormous muscles, amongst other things.

"So J'avet said," I agreed. "Why, what do you have in mind?"

His hand trailed down my back to cup my ass. "I can think of a few things."

"Oh?" I asked teasingly. His touch made my blood hot and the butterflies in my tummy were doing flips. They did that around Slek and Danec. In the couple of months I'd known them, they hadn't diminished in the slightest. If anything, they'd increased.

"Can you cure the Iri?" Danec asked. His expression suggested he'd been thinking hard and didn't realise he was going to speak until he did.

"Cure?" I echoed. "As in, get rid of the nanobots?"

Danec nodded vigorously. Damn, he was cute when he got all excited.

"They could potentially be switched off," Slek said thoughtfully. "But there's a long list of problems with that."

"Like what?" Brinley asked.

Slek counted them off his fingers. "We'd have to switch them all off at once, or more would infest the host. We'd have to find a way to do that, which would require IF support. Then there's the issue of consent."

"Right," I sighed. "The Iri might like being hosts."

"What if they don't?" Danec asked insistently. "They might want to be free."

"If we ever meet another one, you can ask them." Slek patted him on the shoulder.

Danec looked disappointed, but he didn't press the matter. Still, I knew he was thinking about it. He had that look in his eye, like cogs and wheels were turning in his mind.

"In the meantime," I said as brightly as I could. "Who's up for popcorn and some movies?"

"If by movies, do you mean, long, slow foreplay?" Slek asked.

"No. By movies, I mean movies," I replied.

Now he looked disappointed, but nodded anyway. "Sure, I guess I could watch one or two before bedtime." Now his mischievous smile was back.

"I have a training flight," Brinley said regretfully. "Apparently my evasive manoeuvres weren't up to par." She made a face.

"You saved our asses," I pointed out, offended on her behalf.

She raised her hands to either side, palms up. "A pilot can never know too much."

"That's true." I gave her a quick hug. "I'll never stop learning either."

I turned to the guys as she trotted off.

"I have some things I need to do," Danec said reluctantly. "I have classes I have to catch up on."

"Why do I have a feeling you'll never finish learning either?" I asked.

He smiled briefly. "There's always something else to discover about something." He didn't quite meet my eyes.

"I suppose there is," I agreed. I gave him a side-long look, but he flashed me a smile and turned to disappear down the corridor.

"Now that was odd," I said.

"Really?" Slek asked. "I didn't think it was that odd. I mean, he obviously wants to give us some time alone together."

I watched Danec's perfect ass round a corner and shook my head. "I don't think that's it."

"No," Slek said lightly. "He's probably going to look up nano—" He cut off mid-sentence. "Commander Zarex," he greeted with a smile. "I didn't see you coming."

Neither had I. The green-skinned commander appeared almost out of nowhere. With scales on the side of his neck resembling a reptile, he might have the ability to slink. Or I hadn't been paying attention, distracted as I was by Danec's ass... I mean, sudden departure.

I smiled. "Good afternoon."

"Good afternoon Nurse Wright, Engineer Slek." Zarex's voice was smoother than a chocolate fountain and almost as delicious. His slow smile was the kind you might call panty dropping. His antennas, the same shade as the rest of him, bent toward me like a bow, or an attentive listener. Yeah, okay, he was hot.

"What can we do for you?" I found myself asking.

"I need some of your time," Zarex replied. His tone was self-assured, a man accustomed to giving orders and having them followed. Not in the same way J'avet insisted on obedience. People obeyed Zarex because he made people *want* to obey him.

"Uh." I swallowed. "Me?" I, on the other hand, am not so self-assured.

Zarex smiled, a slow, almost lazy smile that made my panties want to twist under my trousers.

"Yes, you, Nurse Wright. Unless you're too busy?"

"Oh, I'm not," I said quickly. I glanced toward Slek, who was watching me, one eyebrow raised. "I mean, we were just going to watch movies, but we can do that later if it's important."

"Oh, it absolutely is," Zarex replied. "It shouldn't take too long, though. I have you back to your…movies in no time." Did he wink at Slek, or did his eye twitch?

Either way, I blushed.

"All right then, Commander. Um…" I shot Slek a glance.

Slek held up both hands. "Go ahead. I'll hunt down some popcorn and warm up the vidscreen."

I nodded. "Okay, sounds good. And don't forget, not so much salt this time."

"And more butter," Slek added.

"Yes, and that," I agreed. Popcorn was always better when it was oozing so much butter it covered my fingers and trickled down my wrist. Okay, it's not the healthiest option, but it was movie night. I could indulge this once.

"This way." Zarex gestured down the corridor, toward the command section of the station. It was generally a place someone like me wasn't allowed to go, except in the company of someone like him.

"Can you tell me what this is about?" I asked. "Am I in trouble?" Just being beside him gave me goosebumps.

"Should you be?" He gave me a slow, sly smile, his eyes half lidded.

I swallowed.

Oh yes, I should be spanked, I thought.

"No, not that I know of." My voice was slightly higher than usual. Hopefully he didn't notice my blush. More than that, I hoped he couldn't read my mind. That would be a touch embarrassing, to say the least. Although, just in case, I thought about what he could do with his tongue between my legs.

"There's a first time for everything," I added. Um, what were we talking about again?

He chuckled, deep in the back of his throat. His antennas quivered with what I assumed was laughter.

"So they say," he agreed. "Often the first time can be the most memorable."

I was sure he meant it to be a completely innocent remark, but my mind took it to a whole new place. I watched him in the corner of my eye and decided his remark wasn't so innocent after all. His smile certainly wasn't.

"Um." Damn, my ability to speak seemed to have fled for a moment. "I guess so," I said finally. *Lame, Edie, lame.*

"Come this way." He waved toward an open door.

Okay, I knew his words were no accident this time. He was flirting, but with more subtlety than Slek. So subtle, in fact, he could easily claim he meant nothing by it at all. I would have to keep my wits about me when he was around.

I stepped into a room with a stunning view of the side of the station, the docks and a hint of Dendra far below us.

Almost entirely green, it was hard to tell the land from the oceans. Truthfully, it looked inhospitable, but was home for a few billion Dendrans and other species.

I turned as Zarex closed the door behind us. I couldn't shake the feeling I was prey, but his expression was benign. For now.

"So." I crossed my arms over my ample chest. "What is this about?"

Zarex circled around the room and stopped at the window. "You saw some of the passengers from Frey-T," the shortened name for Freytauri, "turned into hosts for the Iri nanobots."

"Is that a question?" I asked. "Because you know I did." He had attended the first debriefing on the IF ship which had rescued us from our pod above Calig.

"Yes, I do." He pulled a chair out from behind a desk and propped a booted foot on the seat.

Evidently he didn't plan to offer me a chair.

"I want to hear it again, slowly, and from the perspective of a medic," he said.

"Okay." I pictured the moment in my head before I spoke. "The nanobots looked like a swarm of glitter. I'd hate to get it on the carpet. You'd be vacuuming it up for years."

He cleared his throat.

"Right. Well, they crawled up the bodies of the

Freytauri and crawled up their noses and into their mouths." I shuddered.

"They didn't enter anywhere else?" he asked.

I thought for a moment, then shook my head. "I don't think so. If they did, they went under clothes, so it would be difficult to see."

He nodded. "Why the nose and mouth?"

"I don't know, I didn't know nanobots existed until then." What was he getting at?

"In your opinion," he said slowly.

"Because they're holes?" I suggested. "A way into the brain."

He snapped his fingers so suddenly I jumped. Where J'avet would have found it amusing, Zarex looked apologetic.

"Into the brain," he repeated. He lowered his leg and looked out the window. "All the better to control thoughts and movements."

"I suppose so," I agreed. Now I thought about it, it made perfect sense. They wouldn't be efficient if they congregated in one elbow.

"Did you get any sense of who or what was giving them orders?" He turned and gave me a piercing look.

"No," I said slowly, "but I wasn't looking. A bunch of Iri had weapons on us. I was trying to survive."

"Of course, of course." He waved a hand. "As you should."

"Right. Did they find anything on Calig when they went down to free the other evacuees?" A few hundred had been held hostage so the rest of us behaved when the Iri attacked the Freytauri rogues.

"Signs of recent habitation, but not much else," he replied, which was more than J'avet told us. "It's as if they melted into the trees, but their life signs went with them. They found none."

"Do they have them?" I asked dryly.

He did a double take. "I beg your pardon?" He seemed shocked. For some reason, I found that fascinating. He seemed more—well, not human. Vulnerable.

I replied slowly. "Danec said the Iri aren't dead, but what if the nanobots suppress their life signs? Do their hearts still beat naturally?"

His eyes widened. "Did you see any children?"

My lips dropped apart. "No. Do you think—"

He toyed with one of his antennas.

I wondered what it felt like. Skin? Scaly?

"They have an outpost somewhere," he mused.

"I was going to suggest they're immortal, but that works better," I admitted.

He smiled briefly. "It's possible the nanobots suppress our ability to detect them."

"That would explain why everyone thought Calig was uninhabited," I said.

He looked surprised again. "That's true." He lowered his hand from his antenna and dropped it to his side. "Thank you, Nurse Wright."

"Edie," I corrected.

"Edie." My name sounded nice rolling off his tongue. "I look forward to working with you further on the journey to Agus."

"You're coming too?" I asked, confused. I thought he had a command on the rescue ship.

He smiled. "Someone has to help the captain with the *Halcyon*, and keep Commander J'avet on his toes."

"He'll love that," I said sarcastically. From what I had seen, the pair didn't much like each other. I understood that; J'avet was pretty unlikeable.

"Yes he will, won't he?" Zarex looked completely unruffled by the fact. If anything, he seemed to find it amusing.

I shook my head. This was going to be an interesting journey.

2

"So, what movie are we watching?" I flopped down beside Slek on the wide armchair in front of the big vidscreen.

Dendra Station housed a permanent population of personnel. As such, they accommodated residents and visitors in relative luxury. More luxurious than Moon Station or *Infinity* at least. Both of those were built for function, not fun. With resources sourced from the planet below, the food was better too.

"I found one called *Attack of the Killer Tomatoes*," Slek said. He looked part amused and part confused.

"Oh, a classic," I said approvingly. "And popcorn." Thank goodness corn grew just about everywhere, although it tasted slightly different from planet to planet. Something about soil composition, but I don't know. I'm no farmer. I just eat tons of the stuff, especially on movie night.

"With lots of butter, just as the lady asked." He balanced the bowl on his lap and put an arm around me.

"Start movie," he said.

The vidscreen flickered to life and the movie, bad special effects and all, began.

"What did Zarex want?" Slek asked after a few minutes.

"He wanted to hear about the nanobots again." I told him about the conversation as briefly as I could, with one eye on the vidscreen.

"Masking their life signs, hmmm?" he mused.

"Is it possible?"

He shifted his ass on the seat. "In theory. If we could get our hands on any nanobots, we could find out."

"Whatever could go wrong with that?" I asked sarcastically.

"I didn't mean I would literally touch them," he replied. "But point taken. If someone other than a Freytaurian, or anyone else the nanobots could choose as a host, got their hands on them..."

"Anyone else?" I echoed. "They avoided the rest of us."

"Human, Centauri and Parvoran," Slek said slowly. "We had no one from any other planet with us. For all we know, they'd like Argusians. Or they're currently programmed to seek out Freytaurians, but could be reprogrammed."

"Oh. I hadn't thought of that." I shivered. "Would there be information in the databases that might be helpful?"

"Probably," he agreed, "but if there is, Danec will find it." He smiled slyly.

I swatted his arm. "You're letting him do all the work?"

Slek rubbed his arm and shrugged. "Why not, he's eager. Besides, it means we finally get time alone."

"Things have been hectic, haven't they?" I sighed. "With any luck, the next two days will be as boring as hell."

"Not a chance of that." Slek leaned over to press his mouth to mine. His tongue slid over my lower lip, then the tip split into a fork.

I'd have to remember to ask him later how he did that. Right now though, I kissed him back and opened my mouth to his.

When he pressed his tongue inside my mouth, I sucked on both slender tips. The texture reminded me of a pair of sugar coated sour worms, but there was nothing sour about him.

His hand went to my hip and he gently pushed me until I lay on my back on the couch.

I pulled my face back and asked, "What if someone comes in?"

He chuckled. "Then they'll get an eyeful."

I wasn't sure how I felt about that. On one hand, a thrill of excitement passed through me. On the other, I hadn't been with Slek before and this seemed, well, not special.

When he kissed his way down my neck and started to peel off my shirt, caution evaporated in place of desire.

My shirt ended up on the floor somewhere, then Slek paused. He looked at me in confusion. Or specifically, my bra.

"How does *that* work?"

I chuckled. "The fastener is in the back."

"Oh." He nodded as if he'd known that all along. "Roll over then."

I did as he asked and grinned over my shoulder while he tried to work out the hooks and eyes.

"Ah-ha!" He tugged it out from under me and held it up triumphantly. He tossed it aside and straddled my legs.

While I lay and closed my eyes, he kissed and licked his way from my left hip to my shoulder, then all the way down the right side to the top of my pants. He teased them down and ran the tip of his tongue over my ass.

I wriggled with the deliciousness of the sensation.

"You like that, hmmm?" He tugged at my pants. "You might need to help me out here."

I lifted my stomach and undid the front of my trousers.

"That's better." He tugged them down and threw them aside as well, then did the same with my panties.

"You're a cute shade of pink," he remarked.

"I try," I said while blushing.

He settled himself beside me and traced circles around my bare ass with his tongue. "You taste good too."

He parted my legs gently and flicked his tongue from my rear hole to my folds and around my clit.

I moaned softly.

He flicked again, then ran a hand up my legs, up between my thighs. He rubbed his fingers against my clit and already wet entrance, while his tongue circled my rear hole.

When my whole body started to ache for him, he pressed a finger inside me, then another.

I arched my back. I wanted more, needed more.

He pumped his hand in and out of me, then pressed a finger lightly into my ass.

"You're so soft and warm," he marvelled.

I groaned. "Please," I breathed.

He bent my knee and opened me out to him further. With fingers and mouth, he went to work on my clit.

In moments, I was gasping and grinding my hips against the chair.

On the vidscreen, a woman screamed. I understood how she felt. I wanted to scream the station down.

"Slek," I moaned.

"Yes, Edie?" His voice was muffled.

"Don't stop," I pleaded.

"I had no intention of it."

"Good. Mmmm." I pressed my palms to the chair on either side of my head and closed my eyes.

He paused for a moment, then his fingers were replaced with something bigger, harder. Slowly, he slid his cock into me and sank down deep.

"Oh. My. Stars," he breathed. He kissed the back of my neck, then began to thrust like a man starved of food. Every pound let the massager-like bumps on his cock rub against my clit and all the way through the bottom of my belly.

I was on the verge of coming, but I didn't want to, not yet.

"I want to look at you," I said. "Please."

He thrust another time, then pulled out and helped me to roll onto my back. No sooner was I settled than his mouth descended on my breasts, licking, sucking and biting hard enough to leave marks on my tender skin. Between him and Danec, I was covered in them.

I tugged up the hem of his shirt and helped him out of it. His purple skin covered a rock hard chest with abs to match.

I blinked a couple of times, still unable to believe a guy like him would care about a girl like me, much less want to fuck me.

"What?" He turned his head and looked at me with one eye.

"You're hot," I said.

He grinned. "Yes, but so are you."

I wasn't sure if I should sock his arm or blush. In the end, I did both, but he just laughed and went back to leaving love bites all over my breasts.

I ran the tips of my fingers over his skin, from his

shoulders to his belly. I had seen the size of the weights he lifted. They were twice as heavy as me. No wonder he looked like he did.

I reached down to grip his cock, still slick with my juices. The nodules on his length started at his balls—which looked human, only more purple—and continued, stopping under his head. They massaged my fingers and palm as I worked him with slow, firm strokes.

His hand ghosted over my clit, his touch feather-light, but enough to drive me wild.

I let go of his cock and hooked a leg over his so his tip was poised at my entrance.

We locked eyes in a fierce, intense gaze more intimate than any touch or embrace. In that glance, I saw the depth of his feelings and I know he saw mine.

He licked his lips and slid back into me. This time his thrusts were slower, more deliberate. He wanted, needed to take his time, to let us enjoy each other.

I wasn't sure I could last much longer, but I closed my eyes and savoured the feeling of him sliding out and pounding back in.

The pressure built like a volcano, hot and wet, threatening to blow.

"I'm going to come," I panted.

"So am I." He sounded barely able to speak coherently, like making words was a struggle.

With a cry, I gave in to the whirlpool of desire which whipped me around in a frenzy of pounding blood and pleasure.

He gave his own cry, lower than mine, and thrust furiously. He stilled and I felt his heat rush through me. The warmth made my orgasm last longer and linger in my belly and toes.

I opened my eyes a crack and looked at his face, his mouth opened as he came. A rictus of pleasure and pain, I wanted to capture this moment forever.

He let out a gasp, then resumed thrusting. Just as I wondered if he would come twice, like Danec had when we were intimate, he froze and grunted again.

I thought I was spent, but between his expression and the sensation of his bumps on my clit, I came again too. I had to bite my lip to keep from crying out so loud they heard it on Dendra.

I tasted blood, but it was lost in the cacophony of blood in my ears and the pure fire of my orgasm as it burnt through me without a hint of mercy. Every bit of me throbbed and tingled, ground and bucked to make it last as long as possible.

When finally it faded, it took my energy with it. I

sagged like a rag doll onto the couch and Slek sagged beside me.

"Well then," he half panted, half laughed.

"I hope your first human didn't disappoint," I said, my eyes heavy.

He chuckled, low in the back of his throat. "Quite the opposite. But you would never disappoint me anyway."

"That's sweet," I murmured. "Same to you."

"Of course not," he joked. "I'm awesome."

Now it was my turn to laugh. "Yes. Yes you are," I agreed. "We should probably get up from here."

"Yes." He pulled me closer and nestled down further.

"That's the opposite of getting up," I pointed out.

"Yep," he agreed. "What are you gonna do?"

Before I could respond, the sound of Danec clearing his throat came from near the door.

I flinched and raised my head.

"Um." My face heated hotter than lava. Okay, maybe not that hot, but I had hoped to dress before anyone found us. Thank all of the stars above it was him and not someone like J'avet.

"Oh, hello," Slek said brightly. "Did you find anything interesting about the nanobots?"

I blinked. He spoke like we weren't lying naked on a couch in the middle of the room.

Danec, his face blushed brighter blue, stepped closer.

"No. I mean, yes. Um…" He licked his lips. I could almost see him wondering if he should turn away or not. We were seeing each other, and sleeping together too, but this whole situation was new to all of us.

I saved him the confusion by sitting up and grabbing my shirt. I pulled it over my head and tugged it down to my thighs. It would do for now.

Slek sat up and crossed his arms.

"What did you find?" I asked finally.

"Nothing," Danec said. "That's just it."

I creased my brow.

"There should be *something*," Slek said. "Did you check the histories?"

Danec shook his head. "Even in there, there's nothing. Not even the word nanobot. I tried a translation, in case the word has changed, and still nothing."

Slek scratched his head. "That is strange."

"Could someone have wiped the information?" I asked.

Slek considered for a moment. "More likely

they've hidden it behind a higher level of security. Danec wouldn't have the rank to access it."

When Danec opened his mouth to argue, Slek said, "Neither do I. Given time, we could hack in, but the chance of being caught…"

I sat back against the cushions. "We could ask. Zarex seems to like me."

"Given his questions, it would probably be him who hid it," Slek said. "Or J'avet. Or someone with higher rank than either of them."

"Or…" I paused.

"Or?" Slek prompted.

"Or there's someone on board working with the Iri and they don't want us to find that information."

"Doubtful," Slek said. "The rank they would need to do it would be high. To think someone got in that deep…"

"Stranger things have happened," I pointed out.

"Unfortunately that's true," Slek admitted. To Danec, he said, "You should be careful. If they know you were looking, things might not end well. For any of us."

3

"BEHOLD, THE *HALCYON*." Slek's grand declaration made me smile. "She's something, isn't she?"

I glanced at Danec, who stood to one side of me as I watched the ship's approach through the station window.

He shrugged and half smiled.

Slek didn't seem to notice Danec's apparent disinterest. "State of the art," he enthused. "Out of dry dock only three months."

"She's sleek." I didn't know Zarex was nearby until he spoke. "I'm expecting a smooth ride from her."

Slek managed to tear his eyes away from the ship for long enough to flash a smile. "Finally, someone else who appreciates a fine woman."

Zarex eyed me. "Yes, I do indeed," he said.

I blushed and turned my gaze back to the window

Danec made a face. "I appreciate a fine ship," he said. Evidently the innuendo went over his head. Or he chose to ignore it. "An hour ago, Slek said new ships always have teething problems because the engineer who designed them doesn't fly them, or see to their maintenance."

I glanced toward Slek. "Is that your mother?" I asked.

"It's more than likely," Slek replied lightly. "I've tried to tell her, but she's always off in an orbit of her own."

"The challenge of an intelligent woman, eh?" Zarex said, but he quirked an eyebrow at me.

"Right?" Slek drew the word out, as though he was long suffering. "Can't live with 'em, can't suck your own cock." He placed an arm around me and gave me a squeeze.

"Not unless you're a Centaurian," Zarex said.

Slek did a double take. "Really? I didn't know that about them." He cocked his head. "Hmmm, how about that?"

I cleared my throat. "As fascinating as this is, shouldn't we get ready to board?"

"Yes, we should," Danec said, obviously uncomfortable at the subject of the conversation, and how friendly we were being with Zarex.

I understood Danec's reluctance to trust the Agusian. He was likeable, but he wasn't above suspicion.

Speaking of guys who were not above suspicion, J'avet stepped up behind us wearing his customary scowl. His dark red eyes focused on Zarex, as if the rest of us weren't there. Maybe to him, we weren't. Undoubtedly he was wondering why another commander would bother with the likes of us.

"Ah, J'avet," Zarex spoke before he even opened his mouth. "I was wondering when you'd slink out from wherever you're hiding."

J'avet narrowed his eyes. "Your people are the ones with reptilian ancestors. I'll leave the slinking to you."

"But Parvorans are catlike," Zarex said easily. "I would think slinking is more of a feline thing." He turned to me and added, "Wouldn't you say?"

I ignored J'avet's glare and raised my hands. "Sorry, I'm staying out of this."

"Oh come now," Zarex said. "You're the nurse. In your professional opinion—"

"Enough," J'avet growled. "Are you planning to be insufferable during the whole journey?"

Zarex smiled. "I never plan that far ahead. I merely seize the moment as it comes."

"Then I'll stay in my cabin, just to be sure." J'avet seemed to regret having left it.

For some reason, I actually felt sorry for him. To Zarex, I said, "Maybe we could all be nice to each other and get along?" I gave him a meaningful look.

"Perhaps you should mind your own business," J'avet snapped. He turned on a booted heel and left me to gape after him.

"He's so charming," Slek remarked.

"That's one word for him," I said.

Danec opened his mouth and closed it again.

I suspected he was about to use our nickname for J'avet—asshole-dickhead-prick—but thought better of saying it in front of Zarex. Seeing the two commanders at odds with each other was one thing. Getting in the middle of it, and insulting J'avet, was another. One which might get him thrown in the brig until the *Halcyon* left without him.

"J'avet is a good commander," Zarex said, confirming my suspicion that while he ribbed the other man, he didn't approve of others doing so.

"Did you know the *Halcyon* is the fastest ship of

its kind?" Slek said suddenly. "With a smaller, more efficient engine."

"She'll get us to Agus two days sooner than another ship would," Danec said.

Relieved at the change of topic, I added, "I've heard she has a pretty good infirmary too."

"A full body scanner was installed before she left dry dock," Zarex said.

Did I imagine his eyes raked my body as he spoke? I stood between Slek and Danec, with Slek's arm around my shoulders and Danec's hand touching mine, and Zarex was still looking at me? Yes, I was sure I imagined it. I already had my hands full.

So why did I want him to look again?

"Um. Really? That's... Fabulous." *Very eloquent*, I told myself. It was a shame Kalvix would never see it. The Agusian doctor Slek had flirted mercilessly with was a passenger on a pod destroyed by the rogues. Or so J'avet said. I had no reason to think he lied. He was an asshole, but he was honest to a fault.

"We can scan Danec and see when his balls will drop," Slek said with a laugh.

Danec took a step toward him, outrage on his face. He must have realised Slek was teasing, because he stopped and said, "We can see if Slek has a brain."

Slek looked surprised, then burst out laughing. "Good one. You wouldn't be the first to wonder."

"Because you think with your cock most of the time?" I asked.

"Exactly," he said, with no hint of annoyance.

Zarex shook his head. "I expect to see you all ready to board in two hours." He gave me another look, then nodded to the guys before he walked away.

"Looks like Danec and I have some competition," Slek remarked.

"I beg your pardon?" I frowned at him.

"He's obviously interested," Slek said. "You saw it too, didn't you Danec?"

Danec hesitated before saying, "Now you mention it, yes, I did."

My mouth formed an O. "But I'm so... You two are..."

"We're big boys," Slek said. "A little competition never hurt anyone. I already know you're going to choose me." He puffed out his chest. "If you want to spend time with Zarex before then, I'm okay with it."

"So am I," Danec said softly. "But she'll choose me."

Slek clapped him on the shoulder. "As long as Edie is happy."

"Right," Danec agreed. "We really should be ready to board."

"Yes. Yes, we should." I shook my head to clear it. What the hells? The guys just gave me their blessing to see a third guy if I wanted to. Did I want to? Truthfully, I wasn't sure I could trust Zarex, but I did want to. Then there was the small matter of my physical attraction to J'avet. Yeah, okay, that made no sense to me either, but sexual attraction rarely does.

"At least it won't take long to pack," I said. I had managed to retrieve most of my belongings from the cabin I shared with Brinley on *Infinity*. The clothes I wore when we evacuated were destroyed, just in case a nanobot hitched a ride. Shame, that was my favourite skirt.

"I packed last night," Danec said.

"Um, pack?" Slek said.

I turned my face and looked at him sideways. "Unless, you're only going in what you're wearing?"

He glanced down at himself. As usual, when he wasn't dressed for work, he wore black from head to toe. "I look good like this," he said. "But I'll need my work clothes, I suppose."

"Is this where I offer to help you pack?" I asked.

He raised his head and smiled brightly. "Would you? That would be *great*."

Evidently he'd picked up the word from Danec, who snorted. "I'll help too, to make sure we're not late. The ship won't wait for us."

"It might," Slek said. "I mean, it's us." He gestured, hands straight, toward himself, then to Danec and me.

"If J'avet has any say, they wouldn't wait *because* it's us," I said dryly. "Come on." I took a step, then stopped and pointed at Slek. "We're just packing, though, nothing else."

He held up his hands in surrender, then frowned and jerked his head at Danec. "Why aren't you telling him that?"

"He can think with the head on his shoulders," I said tartly.

"Ah." Slek nodded. "Fair point. Lead on then."

I bit back a smile and slipped my hand into Danec's.

"Are you all right?" I asked him. "We haven't had much time to talk since..." I jerked my head back, toward Slek.

Danec gave my hand a squeeze. "It's a...a new situation. Not something I planned or...or expected." He was clearly uncomfortable at expressing himself. He swallowed visibly. "I meant it when I said I want you to be happy. If that means sharing forever, I'll do it." He nodded several times, then smiled.

Forever. I hadn't even thought about that. The idea was both daunting and intriguing. The guys got along, in spite of the ribbing they gave each other. They were like brothers, in a way.

"And the other thing?" I asked carefully. "The thing you were researching. Has anyone asked questions?"

Danec glanced over his shoulder. If he was looking to see if anyone could overhear, he was about as subtle as shuttle landing on your foot. His innocence was endearing, although sometimes I worried about what the big, bad galaxy might do to him. He had seen people killed in front of him, and almost became an Iri host, and those hadn't changed him too much. He seemed a bit more worldly, but not bitter, not yet. I hoped he never did.

"I had the feeling I was followed this morning," he said softly. "On the way to the shower. When I turned around, no one was there." He frowned. "I suppose it was in my head because I'm expecting something, someone."

"Or they hid before you saw them," I said. "They could have been admiring your cute little ass." I leaned back and peered at it while he blushed bright blue.

"It's not that great," he murmured.

"Nah, she's right," Slek said. "Your ass is adorable. I'm jealous." He gave Danec a lopsided grin.

"Your ass is pretty amazing too," I said before I realised Slek was fishing for compliments. I took the bait, line and all.

His grinned widened. "That's true. Not as perfect as yours though." He slapped my ass lightly.

Now *I* blushed. I turned away to press the buttons on the keypad which would open the door. It slid open without a sound and we stepped inside.

I frowned. "Has someone else been in here?"

"No," Slek replied, "it's just as messy as I left it."

Clothes dotted the floor. A drawer hung half open. The sheets were half on, half off the bed. A dirty plate and cup sat on the table.

"I don't know, I don't remember it looking this bad." I shrugged.

"How do you live like this?" Danec grimaced in disgust.

"How do you not?" Slek asked easily. "I bet your rooms are always spotlessly clean."

"They have to be, I'm in GASP."

The military arm of the IF was as meticulous as

any military, one speck of dust and he'd probably be made to do a million pushups, or something like that.

"Well, I'm not." Slek crouched to pick up a pair of underpants and a shirt.

I pulled his case out from under the bed and opened it so he could toss it inside.

"Do you own any clothes that aren't black?" I asked after he threw in several socks and more underpants.

"I have a white shirt somewhere," he replied. "Not much goes with purple."

"Oh. I hadn't thought of that."

He grinned and I realised he was joking.

"Remind me to swat you on the arm later." I checked my watch. "We need to hurry or we'll run out of time."

"That's the last thing, I think. Oh, wait." Slek grabbed a sock from under the bed and threw it toward the case. He missed by a metre.

Danec scooped it up and tossed it just before I shut the case and clicked it tight.

"If there's anything else, they'll have to send it on," I said.

"Yes." Danec checked his own watch. "We'll have to run. Literally." His eyes were wide with worry.

Slek grabbed his bag and swung it onto his shoulder.

"Come on then, less talking, more running."

I bolted out ahead of him and started down the corridor at a trot.

"How long do we have?" Slek asked.

"Ten minutes," Danec replied.

"Shit." I skidded to a stop outside the room I shared with Brinley. The pilot was waiting outside with my bag and a frantic expression on her face.

"Eight minutes," Danec said.

We dashed to his room, where he grabbed his own bag in about thirty seconds.

"Five minutes," Slek said.

I shook my head. I was already puffing, but I gave up trotting and headed to the *Halcyon's* dock at a dead run. My bag hit me painfully with every step.

I faltered and started to slow. By now, I could barely catch my breath.

Danec grabbed my hand and silently encouraged me to keep going.

"I can carry you if you need me to," Slek said. How was he not out of breath?

"I'm not arriving slung over your shoulder," I wheezed.

Slek chuckled.

We were forced to stop at the door to the docks and wait while Danec pressed his palm against the palm pad beside it.

The palm pad beeped and flashed red. The door remained closed.

"What the—" Danec frowned.

"Here let me," Slek said. When Danec stepped aside, he pressed his palm against the pad. It flashed green and the door slid open.

"See, nothing to it."

"I don't understand," Danec said.

Neither did I. All of our palm prints were on file, as was that of everyone else with legitimate business on the station.

"Worry about it later," Brinley said. "They're boarding everyone."

She was right. A handful of people with bags stood in line at the door. The rest must be on the *Halcyon* already. Beside the door, Zarex and J'avet stood, watching closely.

"Come on," Brinley said.

Resuming our running pace, we bolted to the door as the last of our fellow passengers stepped over the threshold.

"Cutting it close," Zarex remarked.

"Another minute and you would be too late," J'avet said darkly.

"Looks like we got lucky," Slek said easily.

J'avet muttered something and waved us inside.

Zarex's eyes followed me the entire way; I saw him in the corner of my eye.

He followed us in and J'avet came behind him.

The door shut with a soft whoosh, locking us in.

4

"Is it everything you thought it would be?" I trailed a finger down the back of Slek's hand.

"You always are," he replied smoothly. He gave me a lopsided smile which didn't waver when I poked him hard in the back of the hand, fingernail and all.

"I meant the ship, smart ass," I said. "You've practically been drooling since we boarded."

"Who says that has anything to do with the ship?" he asked. He added a brow wiggle to his playful expression.

I cocked my head until he held up a hand in surrender.

"Fine. She's a beauty. Part of me wishes I could stay on her longer." He sighed, then his boyish grin was back. "But then I remember I'd rather stay on you."

I was about to respond when Danec swore at the nearby beverage dispenser.

"Bloody microns," he growled. "Come on."

"We really need to teach that boy to swear properly," Slek remarked.

I chuckled and got to my feet.

"Is everything okay?" I put a hand on Danec's shoulder and startled when he jumped in surprise.

"Oh, s-s-sorry," he stammered, more pronounced than usual.

I hadn't heard him do that in a while. That he did so now was concerning. What had him so anxious?

"Nothing on this ship will work for me," he said. "It's like I don't exist. It doesn't know my palm print, fingerprints or retinas."

"It's a new ship," I said. "It's probably a glitch. It could be that you need to be added into the system again." That was odd though. We had all been scanned and added to the system while on Dendra Station. Yeah, computers still weren't infallible.

I glanced over my shoulder. "Slek, can you do it?"

"Of course I can. Anywhere, any time," Slek replied.

I rolled my eyes. "I meant can you add Danec into the system?"

"Sure, but get the boy a drink first." Slek rose to his feet.

"Oh, right." I looked questioningly at Danec.

"I only wanted a drink of water." He gave the dispenser a dirty look.

"Okay." I put my palm on the pad beside the machine. "Glass of water, please."

A green light blinked. In the front of the machine, a claw lowered a glass and water trickled into it.

I picked up the glass and handed it to Danec, who accepted with a smile and nod.

"All that technology and I can't get a drink of water without help." He looked more embarrassed than annoyed.

"We'll get that fixed," Slek assured him. He jerked his head towards the door before starting off in that direction. "It shouldn't take more than a few minutes."

"Is this a usual problem?" I asked.

"I haven't seen it before," Slek admitted. "New ship, new glitches. They'll probably start to pop up all over the place now."

"As long as the captain and pilots can still

operate the ship, then I don't suppose it's a big deal," I said.

"Yeah." Slek frowned at Danec. He seemed troubled, but he didn't say anything. Instead, he led us into a room full of screens and flashing lights and waved toward a stool. "Sit down, Danny."

"Danny?" I choked back a laugh at the expression on Danec's face.

"Sure. You're Edie, so it makes sense that he'd be Danny—"

"Slekie?" Danec suggested sarcastically.

Slek grinned. "Absolutely. Why not?"

I shook my head at them both. "Let's get on with this?"

Slek glanced around. "It's a bit public, but all right." He grabbed the hem of his shirt.

"Not that," I said, putting my fingers on his hand to stop him.

"Spoilsport." He pouted. "Fine, let's do it." He leaned past Danec and pressed a series of buttons beside a screen. The screen lit up with a series of shapes I recognised as letters and numbers from one of the IF species. Parvoran perhaps.

Slek tapped the screen and it changed to another language.

"Freytaurian," Slek said.

I nodded. I recognised some of the letters and words, but not enough to really read it.

Slek pressed another button and lines of English appeared under the Freytaurian.

"Thank you." I rested my hands on Danec's shoulders.

"Let's see here." Slek keyed in a code and the words 'security recognition' flashed up on the screen. That was followed by a menu. 'Check' and 'New'. Slek pressed 'New'.

The screen narrowed to a circle, with Danec's image in the centre. He twitched.

"Keep still," Slek said.

Danec licked his lips. "S-sorry." He glanced down at his lap, then back at the screen.

Beside his image, his name appeared. 'Danec, son of Jaek.'

Under that came the word 'Unknown.'

A moment later his name came back on screen, then 'unknown' again. They alternated for several moments.

I gasped, "What is going on?"

"I don't know." Slek tapped the screen and it returned to the option to start over. "Sit as still as you can. Edie, move over here, so the computer can't sense you at all."

I moved around behind him and watched around his shoulder.

Danec swallowed audibly, but froze as still as a statue.

Danec, son of Jaek.

Unknown.

Danec, son of Jaek.

Unknown.

Danec...

"What the fuck?" Slek muttered. "It's as if the computer can recognise you, then it can't. You do exist, right?" The side of his mouth turned up, but he sounded worried.

Danec shot him a dark look, but he didn't seem certain himself. "I think I do," he replied. "If I don't, you're talking to yourself."

I snorted.

Slek grinned. "Good point. I might be a little crazy, but I'm not *that* crazy. Yet." He blew out a short breath through pursed lips. "I have no idea why the computer is acting like this. I've never seen anything like it. I'll speak to the computer gwarps and see if they have a solution. In the meantime, you might need help getting food and drinks."

"I can help," I said immediately. "Until we can get

this worked out." I chewed my lip. "This can't just be happening to him, right?"

"Probably not," Slek agreed. "If it's a glitch, there will be several. It might even spread during the journey."

"That's something to look forward to." I grimaced.

Slek shrugged. "The gwarps will be all over it as soon as they can. We can't let Danny here go thirsty." He clapped Danec hard on the shoulder.

Danec winced. "Ouch."

"Sorry." Slek patted him more gently.

"Do you think the scanner would recognise him?" I asked suddenly.

When they both looked at me in confusion, I added, "The new one in the infirmary. It does full body scans. If it doesn't work for him and he gets injured…"

Danec's eyes widened.

"Don't worry," I said quickly, "there's plenty of old fashioned ways to diagnose injury."

"Like you bitching about it," Slek said. "Just remember if you break your arms, Edie is really good at moistening cocks."

I swatted his arm. "I was doing my job."

"I'll keep that in mind," Danec said. "What if I don't break my arms?"

"I'm sure if you asked nicely…" Slek said.

"So anyway," I interrupted, "let's go and do that scan."

"Fine." Danec stood, but his pants bulged. "Then I need to get some study done."

"I'm sure Edie will help you with that too," Slek said as he shut down the computer.

Danec blushed.

I just rolled my eyes at Slek and took Danec's hand as we left the room. "I'm sure we'll figure this out," I said softly. "They'll reboot the computer or something, and it'll be sorted." A ship's computer was probably quite different to a personal one and a reboot in space sounded like a bad idea, but I could be wrong.

"Yes, I know," Danec said. "It's just f-frustrating. If I can't access the computer properly, I'll h-have trouble with my studies. I don't want to fail because of a glitch."

I squeezed his hand. "I'm sure they would understand." I wasn't certain of that, to be honest. If someone like J'avet was in charge, he would get angry, if only for the sake of it.

"We'll let Zarex know and he can send word if necessary," I assured him.

"If I fall behind, I'll have to repeat my classes," Danec said with a sigh.

"You're such a gwarp," Slek said fondly.

"You're pretty gwarpy yourself," I told him.

"Hey," he protested. He paused, frowned and said, "You're right. Don't tell anyone."

I snorted. "Our lips are sealed." I glanced at Danec, who nodded and mimed sealing his lips.

"I think everyone knows though," Danec said. "You are an engineer after all."

Slek pouted. "Hey, I have a reputation to uphold. Player, lover, fighter, badass."

I patted his bulging bicep. "Keep telling yourself that. Meanwhile, we're all gwarps, so you might as well accept that."

"Gwarps and proud of it," Danec declared.

A Centauri man in the uniform of a cook gave us a funny look and hurried past.

I bit back a laugh, but Slek slapped himself on the forehead.

"So much for my reputation. It'll be around the whole ship in an hour." His eyes smiled from around his arm.

"They've seen you with us more than once," I said.

"It's likely not news to anyone."

We reached the infirmary and the door opened automatically.

"At least that's working," Danec muttered.

Slek opened his mouth to say something, but closed it when I gave him a glance. The last thing Danec needed right now was ribbing. Whatever was causing the glitch, it had him worried, or at least frustrated. That was understandable. I would be pissed too if it was me.

I nodded to the doctor on duty and waved toward a bed to the side of the infirmary.

"Lie down and I'll turn the machine on."

"I'm already turned on," Slek said.

I shook my head and ignored his comment.

Danec frowned at him, but climbed onto the bed and stared at the ceiling.

I caught sight of his face in the bright infirmary lights and blinked.

What the fuck?

I glanced at Slek, but if he'd noticed anything strange he gave no sign. He wouldn't have held back if he had seen anything odd. I must have imagined it.

I swallowed back my misgiving and swung the scanner over Danec's feet.

"This will move slowly all the way up to your head." I pressed the buttons on the side.

"The good news is, it can see you," I said happily, trying to mask my real concern.

"That's great." Danec gave me a grin which made my heart flutter and flip. He always had that impact on me. Slek too, but they were both different guys. Slek was a jokester and seemed to think about sex ninety-nine percent of the time. Danec was sweet, smart and probably thought about sex just as often, but he kept quiet about it.

The scanner gave a soft whir and began to slowly move up Danec's body.

Half way up, I stopped it and stared.

"What the absolute, everloving fuck?"

5

Slek frowned. "Is that—"

"What?" Danec looked panicked.

"It..." I sucked in a deep breath. "It looks like a couple of nanobots."

"What—" Danec tried to sit up, but the scanner blocked the way. "You must be imagining it."

"I hope I am," I replied. "There's definitely something moving around in your bloodstream. Two. Three of them."

That would explain the slight silver sheen I had seen on his face. It was gone now, replaced by a paler version of his usual steel blue.

"It's...it's not a computer glitch, is it?" Danec's voice was soft with fear. "It might be them, trying to take over."

Slek took a step back. "No offence, buddy, but those things are contagious."

"Yes, stay back." I waved at him. "But I don't think they're powerful enough to take you over. It took dozens, hundreds even to make the rogues into Iritauri. I suspect three isn't enough."

"Until they make more of themselves," Danec said.

I reached for his hand and squeezed it. "We won't let them do that," I promised. "We'll get them out of you."

"What if you can't?" he asked.

I waited for Slek to suggest he'd be thrown out the airlock, but he didn't speak.

I glanced over my shoulder and saw his expression was almost as scared at Danec's.

"We will," I said to them both. "In the meantime, we should tell Zarex or J'avet." I didn't relish either conversation.

"I should be isolated," Danec said softly.

I hesitated, then nodded. "The infirmary has a room for patients with contagious viruses. It should keep them from spreading into the ship." It wouldn't stop them from cannibalising the metal around them until enough existed to claim Danec as their host. With any luck, it wouldn't get to that.

"Edie." Slek put a hand on my arm and drew me away. "I don't think those things are contagious. From what we've seen, they could eat their way out."

My eyes on Danec, I nodded. "I know, but what else can we do? We need to get them out of him. Until then, all we can do is isolate him until we're commanded to do otherwise."

Slek gave a quick nod. "I suppose so. It's just…"

"I know. You're vulnerable to those things too. For all we know, the whole ship is, if they're programmed to—"

He startled me by snapping his fingers. "That's it." He headed for the door and was gone before I could even ask what 'it' was.

I sighed and turned back to Danec. "I'll finish the scan. It might tell us something useful." I didn't add that something might not be good. I didn't need to, I saw it in Danec's expression.

"Go ahead." He turned his face to the ceiling and closed his eyes.

I restarted the scanner as the doctor approached.

A Garvian, the tentacles on her head stood almost straight up. She must have just started her shift. By the end, they would droop almost to her shoulders.

"Is everything all right?" she asked, her voice high but soft. If she shouted, she would be ear piercing.

I explained the situation as briefly as I could and hoped like hells she didn't panic.

To my relief, she nodded. "The isolation room is the best option, yes. We will work to remove the parasitic invaders from our young friend here." The way she spoke was melodic, like she was reciting a poem, not talking about a terrible threat.

She rubbed a tentacle thoughtfully. "Do you know which metal they cannibalise?"

I frowned. "They seem to like the exterior of escape pods. Apart from that, I'm not sure."

"Ah." She nodded. "Let us follow that line of questioning with the engineers. But first, the scanner is finished."

"Oh, yes." While we'd talked, it had scanned Danec's chest and head. "Everything seems to be normal."

"What does that tell you?" the doctor asked.

I thought back to the conversation with Zarex. "They aren't in his brain. They must need greater numbers for that."

"Possibly," she agreed. "Escort your patient to the isolation room, then inform the ship's command of the situation. I will speak to the engineering team."

"Yes, Doctor." I offered my hand to Danec. For the first time since we met, he didn't take it. Instead he pushed himself off the bed and followed me to the Iso room.

"We can't risk them jumping from me to you." He sounded despairing.

"If they wanted to jump, they would." But I wouldn't press the matter. For one thing, I might be wrong.

I punched in the code to open the isolation room and the door slid open. "I'll put some sheets on the bed and make things—"

"I'll do it," Danec said. "You shouldn't be in here with me. No one should."

I wanted to argue. I tried to think up the right words, but they wouldn't come. In the end, I had to give up and concede he was right. "At least let me get you an extra pillow. Maybe a nicer blanket."

I thought he might refuse, but he nodded.

"Fine. I might as well be comfortable in the time I have left."

"You're not dying," I protested.

He sank onto the bed and tucked his feet up. "I might as well be."

"Hey." I fixed him with a stern look. "We will figure this out. Okay?"

"And if we don't?" he asked.

"I hear Calig is nice this time of year," I said lightly. "I wouldn't mind seeing the moon flowers again."

"You would go with me?" He stared at me in surprise.

"Where you go, I go," I said. "But it won't come to that." I wanted to promise, but I couldn't. I honestly didn't know how this would end, and that made my heart ache.

I tossed him a pillow and said, "I love you, Danec, son of Jaek."

He caught it by the corner and drew it to him. "I love you too, Edie Wright."

I smiled. "Thank you," I said.

"For what?"

"For not calling me Edith." I grimaced.

"It's such a pretty name though," he said. "For a pretty girl."

"We'll have to agree to disagree on those counts." I leaned against the doorframe. "You have a vidscreen in there, with all the latest shows and movies. If it doesn't work, we can operate it from out here. If you need anything else, food, blankets, anything, you only have to ask."

"Right." He squeezed the pillow tighter. "I just want to know I'm not a risk to the whole ship."

I brushed a tear from my cheek and realised I was crying. "Of course. We'll do everything we can to make sure you're not, and that you're not at risk. There are only three, how hard can they be to deal with?"

There might have been one at first. In the time we'd spent on Dendra Station, that one became three.

"Yes, I suppose." He didn't look like he believed a word of it, but he was trying not to give in to his darkest fears. "You should close the door."

I should, but damn it, I didn't want to. He didn't deserve to be shut away from the rest of the ship, alone with three tiny parasitic nanobots which would invade his brain and change him if we let them.

We *wouldn't* let them. Whatever it took, we'd purge them.

Regretfully, I stepped back and watched the door slide shut, blocking him from view. I could watch him on a screen on the wall, but instead I turned to the doctor.

"Doctor—"

"Mazic," she supplied.

"Doctor Mazic, is there a chance the nanobots could be surgically removed?"

"Judging by the scan, they move quickly," she said after a few moments of thought. "We may damage him if we were to chase them about his body. However, in the absence of another option, we may have to consider it."

I nodded. "I understand." The only ways I knew to neutralise them was time outside the body and a laser hand cannon. The cannon would do more damage to Danec than the nanobots, so that didn't even factor on the 'maybe' list.

"You are close to him?" the doctor asked. Her expression gave away nothing of her thoughts. She might be curious, or she may wonder why a hot guy like him would care about someone like me.

"Very close." I ran a hand through my ragged ponytail of curls. "He has to be okay." I wasn't prepared to face any other option, not yet. I would cling to hope with an iron grip and not let go unless there was no choice. Even then, they'd have to drag it out of my fingers.

I turned to look at the screen. Danec lay on the bed, his back to the camera. From the look of it, he still held the pillow in his arms. He was very still. So still I glanced at the monitor which showed his life signs.

Like the one Slek used to recognise him, it flicked between living and not existing.

Limbo.

I swallowed back the choked feeling in my throat before emotion overcame me entirely. I wanted to curl myself into a ball and cry, or better yet, wind myself around Danec and not let go until Doctor Mazic, and whoever else, rid him of the parasites.

I schooled myself into taking long, slow breaths and calmed myself. Hysterics wouldn't help Danec. Only cool heads would.

"Go and tell the ship's command," Mazic said, soft but firm. "Remember your training. Remain focused."

Right. But my training included not getting attached to patients. It was far too late for that. Well then, I would have to fake it, or they wouldn't let me near him. That would break the last of my resolve into a thousand tiny pieces.

I drew myself up. "Yes, Doctor. I won't be too long." I gave a perfectly professional nod, straightened my back and walked from the infirmary so quickly my skirt swished with each step.

A chunk of my heart stayed behind.

6

Technically non-command personnel and passengers weren't allowed in the command area, but fuck that. This was important.

I flashed a dazzling smile at a pair of security guards and swept my palm past the identification pad beside them. It beeped and flashed yellow.

"What is your business here?" one of the guards asked. Their badge read, 'Farnx' and I wasn't sure what species or sex they might be. Their skin looked like it was carved from a lump of jade and they had no hair anywhere I could see. A Dendran, they must have come on board at the station too.

"I need to speak to one of the commanders," I replied. I almost added, 'or the captain' but better she hear about Danec from a commander than lowly little me.

"About?" Farnx asked.

"It's a medical matter," I replied. "It's important."

Farnx and their companion shared a look and Farnx nodded.

"Very well. Go on in. We'll send word you're coming."

I nodded and marched past.

I only made it a few steps when Zarex stuck his head out a doorway and beckoned me over.

"Edie, is everything all right?" His antennas bent toward me as though they too wanted to check up on me.

I waited until I'd stepped into his office and the door closed behind us. Only then did I sag a little and tell him everything. His eyes widened, but he listened without saying a word.

When I finished, I moved toward the window and stood looking out at the stars. They shone and twinkled like nothing in the universe was wrong. Like Danec wasn't stuck alone in a room hoping to keep control of his own mind. Like the galaxy would go on without him. Like—

I wasn't aware I was crying until I sobbed.

I felt the warmth of Zarex's body before he

slipped his arms around me and pulled my back to his chest. He felt so strong, so comforting.

I leaned back into him and let the tears tumble down my cheeks.

"It's okay," he said in my ear. "It's okay. Cry it out. We'll make this right, I swear."

I sobbed for a few minutes, until I gradually began to regain control of my emotions. Or maybe I just cried all the tears I had.

"Shhh. There you go." He smoothed a hand over my hair, down my cheek and stopped at the side of my neck.

His touch made my pulse race.

Fuck, Edie, Danec is in an isolation room and you're getting all hot for Zarex. He and Slek had given me their blessing to explore my attraction to the commander, but the timing sucked.

"I—" I pulled myself from his arms and walked a few steps before turning around to face him. "Danec said there's no mention of Iri in the ships databases. Did you hide it?"

Zarex quirked an antenna at me and an eyebrow to match. "That's a specific accusation." His eyes held a hint of warning.

I stared him down until he lowered his brow and the antenna moved back beside the other one.

"No, I didn't remove or hide any information. In fact, I went looking myself and found nothing. I suspect we really know why."

He pulled a handkerchief out of a desk drawer and handed it to me.

"We do?" I wiped my cheeks and under my nose.

"Who else would have a vested interest in hiding information about the Iri?" He leaned his hip against his desk.

"Other Iri?" It took me a moment to grasp what he suggested. "You think Danec did it himself?"

"Not him, as such, but the entities deep inside him."

Why did I hear innuendos in just about everything he said? Maybe because, in spite of myself, I wanted him badly. Stupid libido.

I cleared my throat. "You think they have that much control over him?"

"What is your professional opinion?" He crossed his arms over his chest and watched me like I was the only other person in the known galaxy.

I shook my head slowly. "We found none in his brain. That doesn't mean they haven't been in there at some point. I'm guessing they don't have the strength to force him to be the host for a swarm of them." I sounded bitter, even to my own ears.

"I can think of three possibilities." He lowered his arms and counted them off on his fingers. "One: they took control for just long enough to wipe or hide the information. Two: they've been ordered to stay out of sight until needed."

"They failed in that, if that was their mission," I said. I gestured for him to continue.

"Lastly, someone else is responsible for removing the data." He crossed his arms again. "Is that why you thought it might be me?"

I shrugged. "You have the rank."

"So do several others," he pointed out.

"You're the one most interested in the Iri, as far as I can tell," I said.

He looked contemplative for a moment. "It wasn't me. There is something else I'm interested in though. Or someone else."

He locked his gaze on mine and stalked toward me.

I couldn't move or look away. Didn't want to. Everything else melted away except him and I.

He slid his palms across my cheeks and around to the back of my head. Slowly, as though time stopped, he drew me to him and pressed his mouth to mine.

Where Danec's kisses were sweet and Slek's were smoking hot, Zarex's felt possessive. As if by locking his lips on mine, he might claim me as his own. His tongue probed my lips, delving with greater persistence until I opened my mouth to let him inside.

Triumphantly, he slipped inside and thrust while I sucked on the soft thickness of his tongue.

His hands moved slowly, but gradually down my back until they cupped my ass. He pulled me to him until the length of my body was pressed against his rock hard one.

I let out a muffled moan. Hells help me, I wanted to climb up him and ride him like a wild horse.

Instead, I forced myself to tear away from him.

"We should… We need to…"

"Right, Danec." Zarex blinked a few times. I guess he wasn't the only one who needed to clear his head. "I'll inform the captain. She'll be the one who needs to make any decisions about him. Her and Doctor Mazic. Uh, and Gaffid, the Chief Engineer."

I nodded. "Yes. Right." My heart pounded and my panties were already as wet as fuck.

Without the fuck.

He walked to his desk and tapped at the keyboard for a couple of minutes.

"The captain will consult with the doctor and keep me informed," he said finally.

"Okay." I exhaled through my nostrils. "What can I do in the meantime?"

He smiled.

"While Danec's whole existence is up in the air—"

"Of course," he said smoothly. "When it isn't, I fully intend to finish what we started."

"I might even let you," I said tartly.

He gave me a look that said he expected nothing less, then said, "Didn't you say your other lover, Slek, said something about nanobot programming?"

"I don't know what he meant by that," I said.

"Then let's find out." He leaned in and kissed me on the mouth, quick, tender, but just as possessive. He meant for me to be his, I was sure of that.

No, my life wasn't complicated. At. All.

"Right. Lead on then," I said. Before we stepped out the door, I glanced back at the screen. "Shouldn't the captain be raising hells about this by now?"

He smiled with one side of his mouth. "Who said she isn't?"

I paused, mouth open for a while, then shrugged. "I suppose I wouldn't know if she was, would I?"

"Exactly," he agreed. "The whole ship will know when she deems it necessary."

I thought he was about to add, 'If she does', but he gestured me out and closed the door behind us.

I caught a glimpse of J'avet hurrying down the corridor in front of us. He didn't slow or glance back. No doubt he was doing something important.

Or something he *thought* was important, I added cynically. I should probably not think that way. He might be one of those who the captain assigned to look into the nanobots. He could be on his way to the infirmary right now to interrogate Danec. Part of me wanted to follow and stop him from being an asshole to my lover. Truthfully, if Zarex wasn't with me, I would have.

But if there was a chance Slek had some answers, I wanted to find out. Needed to find out. Danec was a big boy anyway, he could handle himself with J'avet. Well, as much as anyone could.

Why then, did my eyes follow his ass all the way to the corner? Why did I feel even a shred of disappointment when he disappeared from view? Okay, I knew why. Crazy, stupid lust. In spite of myself, I found him hot. Even with an equally hot and clearly interested guy right beside me and two more who seemed to feel the same way about me that I felt about them.

I shook my head to myself mentally and exhaled through my nose. I needed to focus on one thing right now: Danec and the nanobots. All right, that was two things, but they were intertwined.

"The IF boasts the resources of over a dozen worlds," Zarex said, as if he could read my mind. "We will draw on whatever is necessary to stop the bots."

That sounded so much like a political slogan I had to smother a laugh.

"I know we will," I said. "Danec just looked so…so vulnerable." For a big, muscly dude, he could still break.

"Then, we'll do all we can to ensure he doesn't need to feel that way," Zarex said smoothly. "Especially because you care about him."

"That doesn't bother you?" I asked carefully.

Zarex smiled like the cat who knew the cream was coming. "Quite the opposite. A woman like you has complex needs. I can't possibly meet them all. You need Danec and Slek to satisfy you in the ways I can't. Particularly when I'm busy working."

He stopped and lowered his voice. "A woman like you shouldn't spend a moment unsatisfied, mentally as well as physically."

I blushed so bright I swore my face would catch alight. "It sounds like you have it all figured out." I wasn't sure if I should be flattered, or cranky at him for being presumptuous. Maybe both.

"From the moment I saw you," he said. "I know you felt it too."

"And if I didn't?" I asked.

He smiled as though there was little possibility of that. "Then I would have to relentlessly pursue you until I changed your mind. Or," he added after a moment, "back off and respect your choices." He brushed stray hair off my cheek. "I won't pressure you. There's an attraction there. If you prefer not to explore it, then so be it."

My tongue darted over my lips. I wanted to see where this would go. I wanted to tell him that. Now, however, was not the time.

"I'm sorry," I said softly. When his face fell, I quickly added, "I can't think about this right now. We need to help Danec. After that—"

Zarex looked relieved and nodded. "Of course. He should be our priority. *Is* our priority. And the ship as well."

"Absolutely," I agreed. The nanobots were a risk to everyone on board, not just Danec. He knew that. I knew it too, deep down.

"Promise me something," I said, my tone firm, gaze locked on his.

"That depends on what it is," he said carefully, a smile on the corners of his mouth.

"Promise me you won't jettison Danec unless it's a last resort."

His lips dropped apart in surprise. "I wouldn't even consider it, unless there was no other way," he said. Something in his eyes made me wonder if he was being entirely honest. I realised ultimately it was the captain's call, not his. He could make me all the promises in the world, but they may come to nothing.

"Let's hope it doesn't come to that." He resumed walking and I had to trot a few steps to catch up.

"It better not," I growled. "Or you might have to jettison me with him."

Zarex snorted a laugh, but he said nothing, just hurried his steps.

7

"WHAT DID YOU FIND?" Zarex spoke before I could give Slek a greeting, or warn him we were there.

His face was obscured by some kind of machine which looked like an alcove full of lights. He went to stand too quickly.

"Ouch." He stepped back slowly and rubbed the back of his head. "Warn a guy next time." He gestured at the screen. "I managed to pull the data from the medscanner to analyse the nanobots. I suspect they've been in there for longer than we thought."

My breath caught in my throat.

I gaped at him. "Longer? How much longer? Long enough for him to be the one to push you?" I thought for a moment. "He can't be. He was on Moon Station with me when that happened."

"Yes, he was," Slek agreed. He gave me and then Zarex an appraising look. An eyebrow twitched, but he said nothing.

"How long then?" Zarex asked impatiently.

"Before Calig," Slek said. "If I had to guess, I'd say not long before the explosion that crippled *Infinity*. If that's the case, there was another Freytaurian aboard who let him get infected."

"Or did it on purpose," I said.

Slek nodded. "That too. The good news is, they seem to have minimal programming beyond existing and trying to replicate. The bad news is, that could change and I can't see how to predict when that might be. Or how."

"Can you switch them off?" I asked eagerly.

My heart sank when Slek shook his head.

"If I could get my hands on one, I might. As it is, I'm really only making extremely educated and highly intelligent guesses." He grinned.

I rolled my eyes.

"See, that's a level of arrogance I cannot give you," Zarex said, his expression completely deadpan.

I hesitated for a moment, then said, "Yes, you can."

A smile broke across his face. "Fine, I can, but I prefer subtlety."

"Hey, I can be subtle," Slek protested.

"When?" I asked, then shook my head. "It doesn't matter. Let's save this conversation for later."

"Good idea." Slek turned back to the machine. "As long as they stay more or less dormant, they won't do him much harm. However, they will seek out metal to make into more bots. With only three of them, that will be a lot harder. Many bots make for light work, and all that."

Zarex tapped a finger against his lips. "We need to find whoever infected him. They may have more nanobots."

"They could have infected more than just Danec," I said.

Zarex blinked. "Correct. We'll have everyone use the medscanner. That will at least rule out everyone on the *Halcyon*. Starting with you." He nodded toward Slek.

"I don't *feel* infected," Slek said.

"That doesn't mean you aren't," Zarex said. "Whoever pushed you might have infected you at the same time."

"Assholes," Slek declared.

"They would be, yes," Zarex agreed. "If you're

infected, then everything you told us might be untrue."

Slek looked offended for a moment, but then sighed. "In a way, I hope that's true. Who knows what Danec got up to without knowing it."

"It might be nothing," I argued. "They could have been swimming in there this whole time and nothing more."

"Possibly," Zarex agreed. "Engineer, infirmary. Edie can run the scan on you."

"Someone is going to need to scan me," I pointed out.

They both opened their mouths, but instead of innuendos, Slek said, "I'll scan you after you find nothing inside me."

I nodded and didn't rise to the bait. "You should be scanned too, Commander."

"And Doctor Mazic wanted me to analyse the metal in the isolation room," Slek said. He grabbed up a small tablet from a table. "We need to ascertain its suitability to be nanobot food, then assess it daily for bite marks."

I shuddered.

"You seem competent," Zarex remarked.

"I am," Slek said with no hint of modesty. "I'm sure you are too."

"I am," Zarex agreed.

I sighed. "Is this one of those, 'my dick is bigger than yours' things?"

"He would win," Slek said ruefully. "He has two."

I blinked and shook my head. "I beg your pardon? Did you say Zarex has two cocks?"

"I do," Zarex said, "but Slek's might be bigger than each of them."

I clapped my hand on my forehead. "Two cocks," I muttered. "We really need to concentrate on Danec." But *two* cocks? Holy hells. I glanced at Zarex's groin, but couldn't make out two bulges. "I think I should have boned up on alien anatomy a lot more before I left Earth."

Slek chuckled. "Boned up."

Zarex grinned, but waved us toward the door. "Enough of this, you'll make me blush."

"Like hells we will," I told him. "You might make Danec blush, though."

"She's not wrong about that," Slek said. "I've never met a guy who needed corrupting—" He stopped and looked regretful for a moment before he added, "I mean, leading astray, than him."

"Yeah." I hurried my pace and walked ahead of them. If I discovered who infected Danec, I was going to punch them in the face. If they had a face.

Otherwise I'd punch them in the dick. Or—somewhere it would hurt. No one deserved this, especially Danec. He was the sweetest, kindest, most loyal, with the best ass...

"Hey, Edie." Slek hurried and slipped his hand into mine. "I'm sorry, it was a bad choice of words."

"It really was." I let my hand slide out of his and crossed my arms. "This is not a joke."

"I know. I just deal with things like with, well, inappropriate humour. It's who I am."

I glanced sidelong at him. "I know. Any other time, I might laugh. Not while Danec is all alone, uncertain, scared..."

"Him, or you?" Slek asked softly.

"I..." I looked down at the floor as I walked. "All of those things, I suppose. I care about him. I don't want to lose him. Or you." I dropped my arms and accepted his hand back. "He has to be all right. We all do, you know?"

"I do know," he agreed. "Danec is the gwarpy younger brother I never had." He glanced over his shoulder. "Maybe Zarex is the big brother I never had."

"Only if you remember big brother always knows best," Zarex said lightly.

Slek snorted. "Hardly. Anyway, the point is, we're

a family now. Your worries are mine. You're not alone. If I have anything to say about it, you never will be."

"Unless I want to be alone," I said firmly.

"Yes, unless that," Slek agreed. "Everyone needs some me time once in a while."

"Right." It was strange to think a few months ago, I had nothing but work and me time. I had friends, but we mostly spoke for a few minutes via vidscreen when they weren't too busy with their own work, partners and children. Now I had three hot guys who were into me. I might take the time later to wonder why. In the meantime, I opened the infirmary door and waved the guys inside.

"You know the drill," I told Slek.

Doctor Mazic was off to the side, tending to a woman with a deep cut across the palm of her hand. Another nurse hovered at her shoulder, ready with bandages to help stem the flow of blood.

This was the kind of thing I expected to face day to day in my job, not nanobots and murderous alien species. At least life was never dull.

I turned on the scanner and let it do its thing. Slek lay on his back, hands under his head, eyes toward the ceiling. He whistled off-key as though he wasn't even slightly scared. The hint of fear in his eyes said otherwise.

"I was right," Zarex remarked.

I twitched at the sudden sound of his voice. "Right about what?" My heart pounded so hard it hurt.

"His single cock is bigger than mine."

I rolled my eyes, but I couldn't contain a slight smile at his attempt to lighten the moment.

"Men," I said under my breath. I glanced toward the screen which showed Danec apparently asleep. He looked so peaceful like that, so untroubled. His leg jerked and he shifted. Dreaming, I assumed. I hoped it was a sweet dream. He jerked again and lay still.

"So, what's the verdict?" Slek asked. "Am I bot-free?"

My attention shot back to the scanner in front of me. "It's not seeing any," I said, relieved. "Just some bones which have been broken, but have healed." I knew about his arms, but his ribs had taken a battering in the past, as had one leg.

"Reckless youth," he said. "Lucky I have you now to save me from myself."

"Luckily she has me to save her from you," Zarex quipped.

Slek stuck out his tongue at Zarex.

"Is that any way to treat a superior officer?" Zarex asked.

Slek grinned. "I wouldn't do that to my superior, but I'm not in GASP."

"Just as well, or I'll have to have you court martialed ."

I gestured for Zarex to lie down when Slek vacated the scanner bed.

The scanner restarted.

I will not look at his cocks, I told myself. *I will not look at his—*

My eyes widened. He didn't so much have two, as one which split above the base, like Slek and Danec's tongues. Individually, they weren't as thick as Slek's, they were right there, but it still looked like a ton of fun.

I blushed bright red when I realised both guys were watching me.

"I can't see anything so far," I said. I cleared my throat and tried to push my professional face into place. Considering how hot my face felt, I wasn't sure I succeeded.

I caught a glimpse of something on the screen and stopped the scanner to check again.

"You have a pacemaker," I remarked.

"Reckless youth." He gave Slek a smile. "Actually, it's genetic. My family all have bad hearts. I've had that, or a variation of it, since I was three."

"Oh. Well, it's better than nanobots," I said.

"There are certainly better things to have inside you than those," Zarex remarked.

Slek chuckled. "I like this guy."

I gave him a sidelong look. "Me too. He seems to be clean." After a moment, I added, "Of nanobots." He was definitely dirty in other ways. All the right ways.

"Okay, you can get off now," I said.

"Promises, promises," Zarex said.

"Is everything about sex?" I asked, half exasperated.

"Yes," both guys said together.

I shook my head and climbed up on the scanner bed. "Press the green button and it will start again," I said.

Slek did as I asked and stood back, his hands crossed over his chest.

"I'm worried you'll think I can't be romantic," he said.

"I know you can be," I assured him. "I remember that picnic. Right before we had to evacuate *Infinity*. In the place where you nearly died. That's totally romantic."

"You took her to a place where you almost died?" Zarex asked, his brows raised.

Slek shrugged. "It was the service catwalk above the ship's engines. What could be more romantic?"

Zarex regarded him for a moment. "Just about anywhere. When we're done here, I'll take you to a place I—"

"Wait." Slek pressed the scanned and it stopped just over my belly. "What the fuck?"

I half sat up. "What? What is it?" As hard as I tried, I couldn't see the screen from my angle.

Neither answered. Both stood with their eyes glued to the screen, brows in matching furrows.

"That's strange," Zarex said.

"Very," Slek agreed.

"Would you tell me what the fuck you can see?" I growled. They looked confused and worried. Neither expression filled me with much confidence.

Slek straightened up and looked directly at me. "I don't know how to say this, but—" He looked like a doctor about to deliver a terrible diagnosis.

"Just say it," I said. "I'm a big girl, I can take it." At least, I hoped I could.

I held my breath.

8

"YOU HAVE NANOBOTS," Slek said finally.

I jerked. "I have…" The scan was supposed to be a precaution. I never expected they'd find anything. "But they ignored me."

"That's the strange thing," Slek said. "They appear to be dead."

I exhaled through pursed lips. This got more and more bizarre.

"Can they come back to life?" I asked tentatively.

Slek shook his head slowly. "I think they're dead-dead, but if we can extract one or two, I can get a better idea." He cast me a sidelong look, wide eyes and all.

I could just about read what he was thinking. What if the nanobots had been alive and jumped from me to him? There were plenty of opportunities for them to do that.

"I can extract them," Doctor Mazic said.

I hadn't seen her approach, but she now stood behind Zarex. "It should only take a keyhole and tube to suction them out."

"Can we do it now?" I said eagerly. I wanted these things gone. The sooner the better.

"I have time now, yes," she replied. "Engineer Slek, please assess the isolation room. Commander Zarex, I will inform you when the procedure is over."

He looked as though he might protest, and truthfully I wanted him to stay and hold my hand. However, I knew he was a busy guy. He'd taken enough time for me as it was.

"All right, Doctor." He was all business now. "Inform me and I'll inform the Captain. Engineer, take the dead bots to engineering and begin your assessment. If you find anything of note, let me know immediately."

Slek stopped with his hand on the keypad beside the iso room door. "Sure thing, Commander," he said with just the slightest hint of respect. Enough not to be rude, but lacking enough to make Zarex snort.

"Nurse Wright," Mazic said in that way people

did to let others know they were dismissed and she was taking the conversation back again. "I'll need you to move to the operating room. Luuvor will administer a mild, local anaesthetic."

I grimaced to myself, but rolled off the scanner bed and changed into one of those delightful operating gowns everyone loves so much. I held the back together and climbed onto the operating table, hoping I didn't flash everyone present with a view of my lacy, black panties.

Luuvor, a Centauri who rarely spoke, lifted my gown—flashing everyone anyway— and pressed anaesthetic into my belly with a needle.

I looked up at the ceiling and tried to ignore the sting with each injection. Like most people, I can think of many things I'd rather have stuck into me than a needle. Like—just about anything. I cheered myself with thoughts of thick cocks and double ones, split tongues and hungry mouths. By the time Luuvor was finished, I was ready for a good probing, but not what the doctor had in mind.

She inserted another needle into my belly, this one attached to a long tube and a machine I hadn't seen before. I presumed it supplied the suction.

That assumption was confirmed when she switched it on. The machine hummed for a moment, then made a grinding, sucking sound. Not disconcerting. At. All. Okay, a bit.

Her eyes on a screen, Mazic pressed the needle to my torso and inserted the tip.

"If they are indeed dead, as Engineer Slek suggested, they won't fight their removal," she said. "If that's the case, this shouldn't take too long."

I didn't ask what would happen if Slek was wrong. The tip of the needle was metal. The nanobots would probably munch on it the moment it got close. That idea was discomfiting, to say the least.

"First time dealing with nanobots?" I asked conversationally.

"Indeed. Unlikely to be the last," she said.

"Yeah, I suppose not." Well fuck, that was a cheery thought.

"They're responding to the suction," she said, her tone lacking any expression.

I held back a reflexive flinch. "Responding?"

One eye on the screen, the other on me, she said, "Moving, but not under their own power. They are not resisting the suction." She removed the needle and tapped it on a dish beside her. A lump of black goo slithered out the end.

"That's... more than three," I said.

"Several hundred," Mazic replied. "That's approximately half."

I swallowed back the sick feeling in my stomach. "How many— Never mind." I didn't need to know the total number. "Can you tell how long they've been there?"

"I would suggest they've been in your bloodstream for several weeks." She frowned. "Your body should have purged them by now. Have you felt unwell?"

"No, I've felt fine," I replied.

"I see. They must be designed to have some compatibility with their host, so the body doesn't reject them. However, yours can't give them what they truly needed. Perhaps humans have lower iron in their bodies than Freytaurians, but I am guessing."

That made sense. Something else didn't. "Why not leave me and search for what they *did* need?"

Mazic tapped out a second lump of goo and turned off the suction.

"I cannot answer that. It seems logical to assume they would seek a Freytauri for their host." She rose and snapped off her gloves while Luuvor placed a bandage over the tiny incision.

"Right," I said softly. I nodded my thanks to

Luuvor and rose as Slek appeared to take the dish of dead nanobots.

"Do you want me to carry those?" I offered. I eyed the screen, which now showed Danec awake and looking wistfully at the door.

"I'll be all right as long as they stay dead," Slek said lightly. "Doctor, the isolation room walls are a highly compressed plastic, not metal at all. It might be best to swap out the bed with a plastic or timber one, but he's safe enough while the bots are dormant."

Mazic nodded. "I'll see to that at once, thank you, Engineer." The relief on her face was clear.

"He'll be safe then," I said. "No metal for them to eat."

"Exactly." Slek smiled sideways at my gown. "I like this new look. Especially the back." He tried to peer around while I grabbed hold of the sides.

"I'll get changed and come with you to engineering," I said.

"Or come with me *in* engineering," he said with a sly smile.

"You want to take the risk of there maybe being a live nanobot in there?" I asked. "It might crawl up your cock and live in your balls."

His eyes widened in horror. "I'm sure Doctor Mazic got them all." He squared his shoulders.

"I could get scanned again, just to be sure," I said.

He brightened. "Would you? I've always been in favour of safe sex. And not having ball bots."

"Ball bots bad," I agreed. "Let me get changed first."

I hurried off to do that, before the infirmary got inundated with passengers and crew wanted to assure themselves they were nanobot-free. Hopefully it wouldn't take long. It would be all too easy for hysteria to take hold. When it did, people might start to watch for strange behaviour and point fingers at each other. That would turn ugly fast.

"Okay," I stepped out of the cubicle I'd used to get changed. "Let's do it."

I tried to ignore the dish in Slek's hand as I climbed back onto the scanner bed.

This time, the scanner found nothing out of place.

"Not even a healed bone," Slek remarked.

"What can I say, I didn't start living until recently," I said. That wasn't untrue. I felt as though I lived in a cocoon until I stepped foot on the shuttle and left Earth. I thought I enjoyed life, but now I knew what that really meant.

"That doesn't mean I aim to break a bone," I added quickly.

"But you will abseil the underground caverns of Blarvius with me, won't you?" he asked.

"Abseil?" I shot him a doubtful look. "That sounds more like something Zarex or Danec would be into."

"We would keep you safe," he promised. "After that, we can free-glide off the peaks of Frey-T, and swim in the thermal lakes."

"Now thermal lakes sound like my jam," I replied. I didn't know what free-gliding was, but it sounded terrifying. Not as scary as the clumps of dead nanobots. I didn't know much about them, but I knew broken tech could be fixed. If that was the case, then...

I shuddered.

"Maybe I should carry those," I offered. "Just in case."

Slek had the dish up to his face and was eyeing the clumps with a mixture of fascination and caution. Mostly the former, which was worrying.

"To think, no one has studied nanobots for fifty years since the IF banned them," he said.

"Except whoever made those," I said.

"Well, yeah, but that doesn't count. They did it illegally." He handed me the dish.

I held it at the end of my arm and grimaced. "They're a powerful weapon."

"In the wrong hands, they are. Imagine what we could do with them if they let us."

I arched an eyebrow at him. "Like what?"

"I don't know. Maybe they could break down old ships and rebuild them from scratch. Or crawl into tight spaces to fix engines. Or... Things like that."

"I can see their value there," I agreed. "But I think I prefer they stay banned."

"I guess so," he said reluctantly. "I might be out of a job if they do any of that anyway."

"Yeah, that would suck."

"In the worst way." His gaze settled on my mouth and he smiled.

I was about to say something when the clump slid a millimetre across the dish.

I stopped mid step. "I must have let the dish slip a little." Yes, that must be it.

Why then, did it move a bit more while I stood perfectly still?

"I thought you said these things were dead?" My voice sounded high to my own ears.

"I did. They are." Slek sounded just as worried. "The dish is glass, the lid is on tight. They should be contained in there."

That should fill me with confidence, but in truth I was terrified.

"Engineering or airlock?" I asked. I dared not move a muscle.

"I don't know. We should be able to keep them contained in engineering, but…"

"Yes, it's the *but* I'm worried about," I said.

Slek marched past my vision. The clump moved as if to follow. He pressed a button on the wall and waited.

"Just keep as still as you can, help is coming."

I licked my lips and nodded. "I hope they hurry."

Not a minute passed before the sound of booted feet approached from behind.

"What's the nature of the emergency?" I didn't recognise the voice of the security officer who spoke, I knew the one who followed.

"I should have known," J'avet drawled. "Whenever there's trouble, Edie isn't too far behind."

"Fuck you too," I muttered. "None of this is my doing."

"And yet, you're always right in the middle." He moved around in front of me and peered at the dish. "Activated nanobots."

"It would seem so," I replied. They moved around the dish more freely now. "You're welcome to take them from me if you like. I'm not too attached to them." My hand started to ache with the effort of holding still. No matter how much it hurt, I wouldn't drop them. Not for all the credits in the IF.

"Sir, what are your orders?" The security officer also stepped around me and stared at the dish with curiosity.

"We might never get another chance to study them," J'avet said thoughtfully.

"With all due respect," I said ironically, "if they escape, they'll chew their way through *Halcyon* and enslave every Freytaurian on board."

"I'm not an idiot," J'avet said coldly.

I arched an eyebrow.

"They will be contained in engineering," he said. "Take them there."

"I'm happy to let you do the honours," I said.

"You have them, you can carry them." That was the first hint J'avet was as scared of the robotic critters as I was.

"Your chivalry is touching," I muttered. "Fine, let's go there before my arm gets too tired." I glanced up in time to see a flash of fear on J'avet's face. It gave me no comfort whatsoever.

I took a breath and resumed walking slowly.

9

"For the record, I think this is a stupid idea." I wanted to march the dish to the nearest window and toss it out. If we weren't on a spaceship, with windows that didn't open, and if I wouldn't be sucked out into space, I would. I suspected J'avet would have the security officers stop me if I tried. I might spend the rest of the journey in the brig, while Slek got stuck studying the nanobots anyway. The suspense alone would probably kill me.

Still, I couldn't let it go without giving J'avet my professional opinion.

"For the record, your opinion doesn't interest me," he said coldly.

"I wasn't under the illusion it did," I said, my tone

matching his. "But it had to be said. I bet these good security folk agree."

They said nothing, of course, because he was their commanding officer.

Slek, on the other hand, had no such reservations. "On behalf of Freytauri everywhere, this really is a risk I'd prefer we not take."

"Noted," J'avet said.

"How about that?" I remarked. "He's interested in what another man has to say, but not me."

"I saw that too," Slek said. "The fact you're carrying a dish of live nanobots is a good reason to treat you with respect. One of many reasons."

"Enough," J'avet snapped. "Focus on walking and keeping your hand steady. We don't want any accidents."

"Exactly my point," I muttered. The nanobots were moving quicker now, swirling around the dish like a group of drunk people trying to find the door. "We should move faster. I have a really bad feeling…"

The nanobots tapped at the lid of the dish. They dashed away to the side, gathered into a ball and swept back, tapping harder.

My hand trembled. "I don't think I can hold them."

"Just a few more steps," Slek said.

They slammed again and I swear the lid shifted.

"In here," Slek placed a hand on my back and steered me through a doorway. "We'll put them in the deep freeze."

"Will that hold them?" I asked.

"I fucking hope so," Slek said. "Here, place the dish inside." He opened a hatch on the wall.

I did as he asked and stepped back quickly as he slammed the door shut and hit a button beside it.

The screen showed the dish snap frozen. The glass cracked and the nanobots slid a centimetre or two before they stopped entirely.

I sagged against Slek. "Will that hold them for long?"

"Space is colder and they live there," Slek said. "I think they're stunned. We'll have to work quickly."

"What could go wrong?" I gave J'avet a dark look.

"Fortunately we can jettison them the moment they pose an increased risk," Slek said.

A handful of engineers gathered around to peer at the screen attached to the freezer unit. They muttered amongst themselves, but moved aside when a woman in an IF uniform strode into the room. Taller than me by at least a head, she held herself like someone accustomed to being obeyed.

"Captain Uval," J'avet greeted with more respect

than I had ever heard from him. I sensed he still held something back, even now.

Sexist pig, I thought.

She turned eyes as green as her skin, and slender antennas toward him.

"Commander J'avet. I hear you're responsible for securing a cluster of nanobots for my engineers to observe."

"Yes, ma'am," he replied smartly. He gave me a look as though he wanted me to keep my mouth shut. Fat chance, asshole.

"Engineer Slek and I found them," I said. "With Doctor Mazic's help. He—" I jerked a thumb toward J'avet, "told us to bring them here."

"It was a team effort," Slek said, much more kindly than anything I would have said.

"I see." Uval gave J'avet a speculative look and turned toward the screen. "Curious little machines."

J'avet shot daggers at me with his eyes behind Uval's back and said, "Indeed they are. I understand they were dormant inside Nurse Wright, until they were removed. Perhaps with too much haste."

"Perhaps," Uval said. "They are here now." She glanced at me. "Dormant?"

"I thought they were dead," Slek said. "Either

Edie's system suppressed them in some way, or their programming caused them to reactivate."

"Curious. Well, I won't order them to be placed back inside you." Uval smiled faintly.

"I appreciate that," I said dryly.

"Yes. Well, you might donate some blood for Engineer Slek to test on the nanobots," she suggested. If she wore glasses, I'm sure she would have looked at me over them.

"I'm happy to," I said firmly. "I'll go back to the—" I stopped and felt the blood drain from my face. "The infirmary. Danec! What if—"

"Shit," Slek said softly. "You go, I need to get started on these."

I nodded and started toward the door.

"Commander J'avet, accompany her."

I'm sure he was as happy to hear the captain's orders as I was, but I didn't stop to check. I barrelled out the door and bolted down the corridor as fast as my short legs would pump.

"It won't make a difference if you get there a moment later," J'avet called out to my back.

"I don't care," I panted. "You might not give a shit about him, but I do."

Somehow he caught up to me. It might have been

his much longer legs and higher level of fitness, but I was only guessing here.

"Who says I don't care?" How was he not even puffing? "He's my subordinate, and he's a good kid."

"He's not a kid," I snapped. "He's a better man than you will ever be."

"That's probably true, yes. You won't do him any good if you're winded." He made a grab for my arm, but I swerved to avoid him.

"Don't touch me," I hissed, but I slowed down. "What the fuck?"

"If you can't control yourself, how are you going to be any use to anyone else?" He trotted beside me, his breathing a little heavier now.

"I can control myself just fine," I snapped. Maybe he had a point. I was supposed to be the one who was cool and calm in an emergency. Now here I was, bouncing around like a rabbit in a trap. A cute rabbit, but still…

"Of course," he said. "Is that why I had to tell your pilot friend to get herself scanned after nanobots were found inside you?"

I almost choked on air. I had been so wrapped up in myself, I'd forgotten all about Brinley. I was a crap friend.

"She had none," he said after a moment.

"I knew that," I lied.

He snorted.

"Fine, but I would have told her." When though? When I finally pulled my head out of my ass? When I stopped swapping innuendos with the three guys? I couldn't reason it away. I should have told her first.

"Why do you care anyway?" I asked.

"I don't." He shrugged.

"Sure. You were probably looking for the chance to point out what a horrible person I am."

"As much pleasure as that would give me," he said, "I have better things to do."

"Sure you do," I said sarcastically. "Do you have friends? I've never seen you with anyone." I snapped my fingers. "Except that time on *Infinity* when you told me I was too dumb to play chess. You had someone with you then."

"It's nice to know I'm so memorable," he remarked.

"For all the wrong reasons." Why were we even having this conversation? Or any conversation? What he thought of me was clear enough. "Maybe you should lighten up."

"I'll keep that in mind," he said.

I shot him a confused look. "Right. Okay." He made even less sense than most people. That was saying something.

A shout sounded from up ahead, in the direction of the infirmary. That was followed by a crash. A heavy silence was followed by another crash and another.

"Please, no," I whispered.

"Stay calm," J'avet urged.

For once his words were soothing.

I nodded. "I'm calm." Scared, but calm.

We stopped in the infirmary doorway.

"Bloody hells," I murmured.

Danec was still inside the isolation room, but on the screen, his skin shone silver. In his hand he held the thick wooden leg of what must have been a bed. He pounded the leg on the door over and over. The leg cracked and splintered. With a roar of rage, he slammed what was left of the bed against the wall and tore off another leg.

With this new leg, he resumed his pounding on the door. I saw no sign the door was giving, even slightly, but he kept on until the second leg fell into splinters.

Fuck. The nanobots inside him were evidently

not dormant anymore. Had the ones inside me triggered them off somehow, or were they removed in time?

"Can he be sedated?" J'avet asked.

Doctor Mazic, who stood to the side of the door, frowned. "We can flood the isolation room, yes," she said, her tone as clinical as ever.

"Do it," J'avet said.

"You're not a—" I started.

"The security of the ship is what matters at the moment," he said curtly. He nodded to Mazic who nodded and moved to do as he said.

"Shut the door," J'avet said to a security officer who must have followed us from engineering.

"What the—" I started.

He rounded on me. "Think," he hissed.

I actually took a step back and swallowed. "If the nanobots are active in him, they might be… active in others." And those others might come here.

He waved a hand in my face. "Exactly."

"We don't know if there's anyone else on board with any inside them," I pointed out.

"We don't know there *aren't*," he said. "We're safer here than anywhere, but we need the infirmary intact."

I nodded and my training kicked in. "Doctor, can we scan Danec again when he's out cold?" I resisted looking at the screen. "That's a lot of control for three which seemed all but dormant."

"There's minimal metal in the isolation room," Mazic said, not looking up from the buttons she was pressing.

"Minimal, but not none?" J'avet growled.

"This is a spaceship, there is always metal," Mazic said. "The door handle for one."

"Fuck," I muttered. "He probably had metal on his boots, around the lace holes." Whatever those things were called. Did they even have a name?

"Right," J'avet nodded. "What else? Earrings, rings, pierced dick?"

"No, no and sadly no," I replied. "Zipper. Watch."

"He isn't wearing a watch," J'avet said.

I glanced at the screen. "Not now, no. Why did we not—"

"Berate yourself later," he snapped. "What else?"

"I think that's it. Um, he's wearing pants."

J'avet frowned at me.

"His zip must be intact. The button too. There's more metal in with him they haven't eaten."

"Good. As soon as he's asleep, we'll remove it and scan him."

"What could go wrong?" I muttered.

"Everything," he agreed.

My heart stopped. "How far are you prepared to go if this goes badly?"

The expression on his face made my blood run cold.

"HE'S ASLEEP," Mazic declared.

"Are you certain?" J'avet asked.

Mazic hesitated.

"Be sure," J'avet warned.

"He is unconscious," Mazic said firmly. "He'll stay that way if he's left where he is, so we need to hurry."

J'avet nodded and unlocked the door to the isolation room. Danec had slumped against the door and now flopped to the floor.

"Grab his boots." J'avet crouched and started undoing Danec's trousers. "Hurry."

I crouched and grabbed Danec's boots. I tugged them off and shoved them into a plastic box Luuvor held. I slid my hand under his ankle and helped J'avet slide his pants off, one leg at a time.

"That should be it," I said.

"Everyone out then." J'avet dropped the trousers into the box and Luuvor snapped the lid shut.

I gave Danec's sleeping face a quick, regretful look and followed the others out.

J'avet closed the door behind us.

Mazic started the scanner which would read the entire isolation room.

"This will take some time," she said. "It's not as specific as the new body scanner, but should give us a good idea of the situation."

J'avet nodded. "Body scans for everyone else. No one leaves the infirmary until they're clear of nanobots." He paused for a moment, then added, "Scan that box first."

I stood beside Mazic, rocking on my feet with a mixture of impatience and fear.

"There are certainly more parasites than before, and more active." She could have been talking about the menu for the night's meal, she sounded so bland. "If we could freeze them, we might remove them."

"If we do that, we might kill him," I said with a sniff.

"We might not have a choice," J'avet said over my shoulder.

I turned to glare at him. "I'll go in there with him

and try to extract them myself, if I have to," I said. "I won't give up on him."

"If it's him or the ship…" J'avet said.

"It's not there yet." I paused. "You would really destroy the ship if you had to, wouldn't you?"

"To save the IF, I would," he agreed. "You should be ready to make that call if necessary."

"Me?"

"You." His hand swept across the room. "Doctor Mazic, all of us. If we have to make the sacrifice, we will."

I stared at him until he frowned.

"What?"

"Would blowing the ship up kill the nanobots?" I asked.

"Technically, they're not alive—"

I scowled.

"I don't know," he admitted.

"Seems we should find out before we kill ourselves then," I said bluntly.

J'avet looked thoughtful and nodded. He walked to the comms panel on the wall and spoke to someone in engineering.

"Controlled experiment. Small explosion. Yes. As quickly as you can."

I only caught snatches of the conversation,

enough to understand. Slek's voice on the other end was soothing.

I jumped at a sudden banging on the door. I backed away, half expecting it to crash open. An army of Iri, with silver faces and glazed eyes, would pour in and eat our brains—

Oh wait, that's zombies. Iri have a normal diet of fruit, vegetables and fish. Still, when the pounding came again, I looked around for something to use to defend myself.

"Let me in," a voice came from the other side of the door. Specifically, the comms beside the door, which delivered the sound into the infirmary.

"Zarex," I said with some relief.

J'avet scowled. The two men seemed to hate each other with a passion, although I didn't know why. Maybe because Zarex was nice.

"What is your status?" J'avet replied. He hadn't moved from the comm panel.

"Nanobot free, as of the last scan," Zarex said. "I have someone here who requires medical assistance."

I thought J'avet might refuse, but he nodded to the security officer who opened the door.

Zarex stepped inside, his arm around Brinley, who looked dazed. Blood covered her forehead, but it had already begun to dry.

I hurried forward, but J'avet waved me back.

"Scans first, then we decide if you're welcome or not," he said coolly.

"It's good to see you too, J'avet." Zarex smiled. It broadened when he saw me, but then his attention was on helping Brinley onto the scanner bed.

"What happened?" I asked from a safe distance.

"We met an Iri," she said weekly. "He tried to get onto the bridge. We managed to push him into an escape pod and eject it, but..."

"They have a whole pod to devour," J'avet said darkly.

"With any luck, they'll deactivate before they meet anyone," Zarex said, but he didn't seem confident of that.

"No nanobots," I reported when the scan was finished. I helped Brinley off and gave her a hug before Zarex climbed up in her place.

"We really need a handheld version," I said. I led Brinley over to a cubicle and started to clean up the gash in her head. "How are you feeling?"

"A bit wobbly," she replied. "I didn't lose consciousness and I don't feel like vomiting."

"Good. Those would have been my next questions." I smiled briefly and wiped away the last of the blood. "That sounds like it was scary."

She shivered. "It was. He was nothing like the relatively nice Iri on Calig."

"You mean the ones who wanted to turn every Freytaurian into one of them?" I asked ironically.

She snorted softly. "Yes, them. At least they weren't violent. Except Selvia."

"I didn't see any of her companions try to stop her," I said. That made them just as bad, in my book. "I know what you mean though. Danec tried to break the door down."

For the first time, she noticed him out cold in the isolation room. Her mouth formed an O.

"Shit, this has all gotten out of hand, hasn't it?" She frowned and winced. "Ouch."

"Sorry." I finished a last swipe and reached for a bandage. "You'll need to lie down and rest for a while."

"That might teach her not to be too heroic next time." Zarex placed a hand on my shoulder.

When I glanced at him, he smiled. "Still bot-free."

"That's good. What do you mean by heroic?" I asked.

"She did the shoving while I held the door open," Zarex said.

"Pfft," Brinley replied. "We both shoved."

"Yes, but only one of us got hit by a chair leg," Zarex said.

"I should have ducked faster," Brinley said.

"You distracted him long enough for a last shove into the pod," Zarex said.

"It sounds like you both deserve a medal," I told them.

Brinley beamed.

Zarex simply shrugged. "All in a day's work. Now here we all are."

"Except Slek."

The moment I said his name, the comms buzzed.

"Engineer Slek here. A single nanobot can be destroyed by explosion. A cluster, however, is harder."

"Define harder," J'avet snapped into the comm panel.

"The ones on the outside protect the ones on the inside," Slek said calmly. "If I had to guess, I'd say they cannibalise and re-assimilate the metal, if they can reach it. A laser will destroy a cluster."

We knew that already, but lasers weren't recommended to be taken internally.

"So we can't destroy the ship," I said. "Unless we laser the whole thing."

"That would take a shit load of laser power," Slek said.

"Or a laser cannon hooked up to the weapons array," J'avet said.

"Which will only work if it's on another ship," Slek said.

"Wonderful," I muttered. "We can't self destruct, but someone can do it for us."

"Only as a last resort," Zarex said. He put an arm around me and drew me close.

"What do we do with Danec?" I asked. "We can't laser him." I glared at J'avet, in case he planned to suggest such a thing.

"They were dormant inside you," Zarex said slowly. "Was that you, or a coincidence?"

"If anyone can put someone to sleep, it's me," I said, trying to joke but falling flat.

"Has anyone tested your blood to see if it has some impact on them?" Zarex asked.

"Not yet," I said. "But I'm not sure how that will help Danec."

"Let's figure that out when we get to it," Zarex said firmly. "We need a vial of your blood and a vial of Freytauri. And some nanobots."

"That can be arranged." I nodded. I went to step away.

"Wait," Zarex said. "And a vial of Brinley's blood. To see if it's a human thing."

"It might be a programming thing," I warned him.

"At least we can rule out another angle," he said. "That will get us closer to an answer."

I nodded and beckoned to Luuvor to take my blood and Brinley's.

"We'll need a vial of Slek's as well," I said, the precious blood held in my fingertips. "Don't tell me, we have to go back to engineering."

Zarex tapped a finger against his lips while J'avet glared at him.

"The medical equipment is here," Zarex said finally. "Engineer Slek will have to bring himself and a dish here. We'll need some equipment." He crouched and started to look through cupboards. Finally he pulled out a few glass dishes, some beakers and a microscope.

"It has metal on it, but that can't be helped." Zarex looked toward the door. "Where is Engineer Slek? He should be here by now."

I jerked. "You're right. That's odd."

J'avet tapped the comm panel, but got no response. He shook his head. "I'll try engineering. Perhaps he hasn't left yet."

We waited, collective breath held.

Nothing.

"I'll try the bridge." J'avet looked impatient now. "Come in. Captain? Anyone? Any personnel aboard *Halcyon*, respond."

The silence made my ears ring.

"I guess the comms are down," Brinley said uneasily.

"That could be it," I replied. I hoped to hells that was all it was. "What do we do now?"

"Same as we already planned," Zarex said. "We'll need to take live nanobots out of Danec and test them."

"Have you lost your mind?" J'avet snarled. "Bringing them in here at all would be sheer insanity, but at least if they arrive frozen—"

"What else do you suggest?" Zarex asked pleasantly.

"We get ourselves a few laser guns from the weapons store and fight our way to a pod, then wait for the IF to laser *Halcyon* out of the sky," J'avet snapped.

"And leave Danec to die?" I asked, furious.

"Better him than all of us," J'avet replied.

"Coward," I hissed.

For a moment, I thought he might hit me, but he growled and turned away instead.

Heart racing, I curled my lip at his back and took a deep breath.

"Doctor Mazic, can we safely remove a nanobot or two from Danec?" I asked.

"Safely?" She looked doubtful. "We can try, but we'll have to stay in the isolation room while we work. Including studying them under the microscope."

I nodded and held up the vials. "Let's do it." My back straight, I grabbed a mask so the gas which lingered in the iso room wouldn't put me to sleep too, and marched to the isolation room door. Mazic and Zarex were right behind me, each with a mask of their own.

"You don't have to come," I said to Zarex.

"Oh, but I want to," he said smoothly.

I glanced past him. J'avet paced across the room and back again, muttering to himself. "If this doesn't work, we'll try your way," I said.

He glared daggers at me. "If that doesn't work, it will probably be too late."

I nodded. He was probably right, but if human blood could do anything…

The door slid shut behind us.

Mazic held a small hand scanner and a long needle. "We can't risk the suction machine," she said.

I wasn't sure we could risk the needle or scanner, but we had little choice at this point.

Mazic crouched beside Danec and waved the scanner over his middle. "I'll be guessing here and we'll have to work fast."

She slid the needle into his middle and drew back blood and hopefully bots. She smeared a few drops on a microscope slide and handed it to me.

I slid it under the microscope and put my eye to it.

"What the fuck?"

11

"WHAT IS IT?" Zarex asked.

Before I could answer, I took another long look. "I've never seen anything like it." For some reason I had expected to see a microbe, like a virus particle. What I saw instead was a robot—no, an android—in microscopic detail. I would almost swear they looked back at me.

"So long, sucker." I undid the vial containing my blood and let a drop fall onto the slide. I closed the vial and put my eye back to the microscope. At first, I didn't think anything was going to happen. Then the nanobot jerked and tiny limbs stretched out before they retracted and it fell over and lay still.

"Yawned, stretched and fell asleep," I muttered.

"Not just its programming then," Zarex said.

I jumped. I hadn't realised he'd moved and his face was right beside mine.

"I suppose not." I gave him a watery smile and moved aside to let him look.

"Here's another." Mazic shoved a slide toward me. "Try the pilot's blood."

I slid out the first slide and repeated the experiment. As with mine, the nanobot became dormant with Brinley's blood.

"Let's try with Danec's," I said. I was well aware we were running out of time. Even as the doctor inserted the needle, he twitched violently.

She handed me a vial with only a few drops.

I smeared some on a slide and checked it before I added it to one with nanobots. No point in adding them if they were already there.

As I expected, they didn't fall dormant when they were doused in Danec's blood. If anything, they became more animated, like a child splashing around in water on a hot day.

Just for shits and giggles, I added some of my own blood. The response was slower this time, but they eventually shut down like the others.

"This is great," I said, "but we don't know if adding human blood to Freytauri bloodstreams might kill them."

"I'm not sure we have a choice," Zarex said.

I looked to Mazic, who nodded.

"It's never been done that I'm aware of, but if we can make the bots dormant, I can extract them."

I nodded. "All right then." I handed the vials of human blood to Mazic and took the scanner she held out to me.

"Show me where and I'll inject him," she said.

I licked my lips and held the scanner over Danec's middle. For all we knew, they could be all over his system, but we had to start somewhere.

Mazic prepared a fresh needle and inserted it into Danec, just below the scanner. The moment she finished depressing the plunger, his back arched. She managed to pull the needle free before he kicked out. She rolled out of the way, eyes wide.

Danec's back arched again and he let out a piercing scream which sliced my nerves in half. He kicked out with both legs and his arms flailed. He narrowly missed hitting me in the face with a hand.

"We need to hold him down, for his own safety," Mazic said. "The gas isn't sufficient to contain him."

Zarex scooted over to grab both of Danec's ankles, while Mazic and I gripped a wrist each.

I held on with everything I had, my eyes focused on Danec's face. For approximately a century, he didn't look like one of the guys I cared about. He looked like a wild beast. Eyes white, mouth frothing, jaw clenched with the effort of fighting us, or fighting the nanobots.

"Come on, babe," I said firmly. "You can do this. We can do this." *Please don't let us have killed him.*

His eyes snapped closed and the skin on his face turned entirely silver. The colour crept into his hair, bit by bit.

"Nonono." My vision blurred with tears. We must have made the nanobots fight harder to get control of him. Of *course* we had. In trying to save him, we had condemned him, turned him into a host.

I let out a sob, and managed to cling on while he gave one last furious thrash.

Then he flopped, completely still.

"Danec?" I blinked away tears.

An expression of utter calm came over his face. He smiled.

Shit.

Shit. Shit, Shit. And *fuck* for good measure.

His face went slack and his head rolled to the side. The silver colour drained out of his face and in a heartbeat it was completely blue again.

"What the—" I shook my head. Before I could say another word, or fully grasp the situation, Mazic jammed yet another needle into Danec and was busy sucking dormant nanobots out of his system.

"Nurse, scanner," she ordered. "Commander, get that glass dish over there. No, over there. Open it and hold it."

In the corner of my eyes, I saw Zarex nod. He picked up the vial of Brinley's blood and emptied the contents into the dish before he held it out to Mazic.

Good thinking. If they stayed drenched in blood, they may remain dormant indefinitely.

Clump by clump, Mazic pulled nanobots out of Danec and squirted them into the dish.

"Scan over here," Mazic ordered. She nodded toward Danec's right hip.

I did as she asked and winced at how close several bots were to his bone.

Mazic pursed her lips and moved slowly and carefully. At one point, she winced and Danec twitched. She must have grazed bone, but any pain he suffered later would be better than bots.

"Scan his head and chest." Mazic sat back and wiped her brow with her sleeve.

I did as she asked. "Clear." Anticipating her next words, I scooted down to scan his groin—no ball bots—and his legs and feet.

"Right heel," I said finally. "It's moving like crazy."

"Too far from where the blood was administered," Mazic said. "I'll have to try to isolate it."

I hoped by that she didn't mean cut off his foot.

Instead, she grabbed a tourniquet out of her bag and wound it around his ankle. She pulled it tight.

"As soon as it's out, pull that off," she said. "We don't want to cut off the blood flow for too long, just enough so the little bastard doesn't escape." Did she have to sound like she was enjoying herself quite so much?

I pursed my lips and nodded. "Yes, Doctor." Scanner in one hand, I kept the other near the tourniquet.

Brow creased in concentration, Mazic slid a new needle into Danec's heel, a smaller one this time. The others she discarded into a plastic dish.

"Come here, you little bastard," she muttered.

I moved the scanner around to follow the bot, while trying to avoid getting in the doctor's way. Several times, I had to switch position so she didn't end up in my lap.

"Gotcha!" she said suddenly and right beside my ear. She pulled the needle free and dropped the whole thing into the dish of blood.

"Take off the tourniquet."

I unclicked and whipped it clear as quickly as my trembling fingers could manage.

Mazic leaned back and rubbed her face. "He should be bot-free, but that won't be feasible to do to every single person they get inside."

"We'll figure out something." Zarex snapped the lip on the dish. "We should get these to engineering. They can freeze them and we can go from there."

Mazic nodded. She looked tired.

I was exhausted. I leaned down to rest my head on Danec's chest. "Now we have to wait for him to wake up," I said. To go through all of that, only to lose him, would shatter my heart into a thousand pieces.

"Yes. We can move him into the infirmary now," the doctor said. "It will be easier to monitor him there."

Zarex nodded and rose. He carried the dish to the door and tapped on it.

"We've finished the procedure, you can let us out now," he called out. The isolation room had no comms panel, but doubtless J'avet was monitoring.

That was confirmed when his voice came from the speaker in the ceiling.

"How can I be certain none of you poses a risk?" he asked.

"Because I said we don't," Zarex called out pleasantly. He tapped on the door again.

"A moment," J'avet said.

Zarex frowned. He looked back toward me and shrugged.

The minutes dragged on.

Zarex knocked on the door again. He seemed increasingly uneasy.

Finally, the door slid open. J'avet stood a couple of metres back. "You ask me to put the rest of the ship at risk," he said coldly, "at least give me time to retreat all the other personnel to the far side of the infirmary."

"Good thinking," Zarex said nicely, maybe ironically. I was too tired to tell the difference. "I come bearing nanobots. Don't talk too loudly, they're asleep."

"Your humour is as hilarious as ever," J'avet said, with no hint of mirth whatsoever.

"I thought so," Zarex agreed. "We'll need help moving the ensign into the main infirmary." He jerked his head back toward Danec.

When J'avet looked uncertain, I said, "We can use the body scanner again, if you're scared."

J'avet's eyes flashed. "Do that," he snapped.

Personally, I'd be happy if I never touched the machine again, but I nodded.

As Luuvor and the security officer moved to pick up Danec, I rose and stretched my protesting muscles. When this was over, I would sleep for a week.

I let out a soft breath. With Danec bot-free, and the nanobots off to the deep freeze, I supposed it was over. Or, it would be when he awoke.

I took a quick moment to check on Brinley, who had apparently slept through the whole thing. Lucky her.

All I needed now was to know Slek was safe.

"There's still no answer from the bridge," J'avet said as Zarex stepped toward the door.

"That's concerning," Zarex said. He didn't sound worried, but he looked it.

J'avet snorted. "We need to find out what's going on up there."

Zarex glanced down at the dish in his hand, then back up again. "Engineering first, then the bridge. We should go together."

J'avet nodded without hesitation. He gestured toward the security officer. "You're with us."

To Mazic, he said, "You're in charge here." As if she wasn't already.

Mazic looked unimpressed, but nodded. "We'll be fine here. Nurse Wright, accompany the commanders in case anyone is in need of medical attention."

My lips dropped apart. I looked toward Danec, who was being lifted from the scanner bed to one in the cubicle. Free of nanobots, just like I'd said. I didn't bother to shoot J'avet a triumphant look, that would be petty. Okay, maybe I gave him a small one.

He ignored it.

"I'll keep an eye on him," Mazic assured me. "And the pilot. Your skills are needed elsewhere."

I nodded. There was no point in arguing. She was in charge of me, so I had to follow her orders. Besides, she was right. There might be injured people on board, incapable of reaching the infirmary. I didn't want to think why that might be.

"Yes, Doctor."

J'avet looked less than pleased, but Zarex gave me a reassuring smile. He reminded me that he was hot, and later we might get to have some bot-less, clothes-less fun. That thought helped to push the tiredness away.

I followed Zarex to the door and waited while J'avet pushed the button to unlock and open the door.

The moment it slid aside, the sound of screams

echoed up the corridor. Pain, rage or fear, I couldn't tell. Maybe all of them.

"Edie, walk between us," Zarex said. He stepped in beside me.

"I have a bad feeling about this," I whispered.

"Me too," Zarex said.

In silence, we started down the corridor, inching closer and closer to the source of the scream.

12

WE MADE it a handful of steps before the scream came again. Louder this time, it sounded male.

Fear crept up my spine like a spider, crawling, tickling until I had to hold back a wave of panic.

Get it together, Edie, I told myself. *You've already been through enough already and you're okay. Whatever this is, you'll be fine.*

I sucked in a breath, but squashed myself down a bit more behind J'avet.

Because of that, I almost ran into him when he stopped suddenly.

"Zarex, you and Edie go around to engineering. I'll deal with whatever is going on ahead of us."

"This is a quicker route," Zarex said. "There's no

guarantee we won't meet trouble if we go the long way."

"Are there service shafts we can crawl through?" I asked.

They both looked at me funny.

"No," J'avet replied after a moment. "Only in Earth movies."

"Then how does anyone access the inner—"

J'avet put a hand over my mouth. "Quiet, or you'll get us all killed." He moved his hand and I glared at him.

I wanted to tell him that if he ever did that again, he'd find my knee in his groin. Now, however, wasn't the time.

"We're staying together," Zarex said firmly.

J'avet gave a long-suffering look and turned away.

At least I know it's not just me he hates, I thought. *He doesn't seem to like anyone, including himself. He must be lonely.* I almost felt sorry for him. Almost.

"I believe the sound came from the galley, sir," the security officer said. He was a tall man, with yellow-green skin. I couldn't tell if he was Centauri, Agusian, a combination or another species altogether.

J'avet nodded sharply.

I almost suggested a cook burnt themselves, but I bit my tongue. With any luck, that was all it was. Burns were easy to heal these days. Instinct told me it was something much worse.

We moved toward the open door to the galley, feet silent with our cautious steps.

Sweat broke out on my palms and under my arms.

Zarex put a hand on my shoulder and gave me the dish.

"Stay out here and keep this safe," he mouthed.

I nodded, although I didn't want to stand out here alone. I hugged the dish to me and hoped the nanobots would remain dormant.

The three guys stepped through the doorway. After a moment, I leaned in so I could see inside.

I held back a gasp.

Bodies lay on the floor, blood pooled around them. One, no two, were dressed in the white uniforms of ship cooks. Both were Agusian. Two security officers, both Parvoran, held blasters. One's arm hung at his side and his sleeve was covered in blood.

What caught my eye was a woman who lay on the floor, a gaping wound in her chest. Her skin was silver. In her hand, she clutched a huge carving knife.

"Edie," Zarex said slowly, "get the dish to engineering. *Now.*" He backed toward the door, toward me.

I nodded. I didn't wait for Zarex before I trotted off. It would only be a matter of time before the nanobots inside the woman fled her in search of more bots, or Freytaurians. We didn't need them to appropriate the ones in my hand.

I made it a handful of steps before a couple of Iri came around the bend in the corridor.

I stopped dead.

Shit, fuck and more shit. My eyes widened and my grip on the dish tightened so hard I thought it might crack. I loosened it just slightly. *Don't drop it*, I told myself.

Both Iri wore IF uniforms, one of a security officer. The other from the ship's laundry. Wasn't washing other people's dirty clothes bad enough without *this* happening to them? Fuck knows I hated doing the job, and that was just my own clothes.

"Uh, hi." I raised my hand and gave a little wave. "I'm not Freytauri, as you can see, so I can't host your little friends. Sorry about that." I shrugged one shoulder and smiled sweetly. "If you don't mind, I'll just be on my way."

They looked blank, like computers waiting to boot up, or a remote control car before the operator moved the switch.

Waiting for programming? That would imply someone else was on the end of all of this. Who or where they were, I didn't know. Couldn't guess. They could be on board, or on the other side of the galaxy for all I knew.

They stepped forward, almost in unison. I half expected them to shuffle like zombies, but they moved as naturally as they would without the nanobot infestation. Not the living dead then. More like the living infested.

I swallowed. They couldn't make me a host, but they could kill me and I was pretty sure the security officer was armed.

"I mean you no harm." I took a step back.

"You will come with us," the laundry worker said, so pleasantly they could be inviting me for a picnic, or something equally fun.

"I'd love to," I said regretfully. "But I can't. I have to meet a friend. A good friend. He'll wonder where I am if I'm late." I glanced at my watch. "Look at the time. I'm *already* late. Sorry guys."

I took a step to the side, but found a blaster in my face.

"You will come with us," the security officer said.

"On second thought, I could spare some time." I couldn't guess what they wanted with me, unless the nanobots in the dish were little snitches who told what human blood could do. I thought rude thoughts at them. Wasn't trying to take over one of my boyfriends bad enough?

Wait. Boyfriends? When did I start thinking about them that way?

Anyway, focus, Edie.

"Where are we going?" I asked.

"Turn around and walk," the security guy said reasonably. He stepped away from the laundry worker.

Rule number one, never let anyone take you to a second location. I remember my mother telling me that. I wasn't sure if it applied here, but what the hells.

I popped open the lid to the dish and tossed the contents into the security guy's face. He jerked back.

I wasn't sure what happened then, because I turned like a cute little rabbit and ran like hells.

I bolted around the bend and almost collided

with J'avet. I skidded to a stop and he grabbed me before I could trip over my own feet. Or his.

"Iri," I said simply.

He shoved me behind him so fast I almost fell for the second time in as many minutes.

Zarex grabbed me this time and pulled me to him. He held me close while the three non-Iri security officers pulled their blasters and faced back down the corridor.

"The dish?" Zarex asked.

I winced. "I might have thrown it to slow them down. I figured human blood and all..."

"You're safe. That's what matters." He kissed me quickly on the mouth, then stood with a protective arm around me.

Blasters flashed and the laundry worker—it sounded like him—cried out.

J'avet shouted something and my heart skipped.

No, I totally didn't care if he was hurt. Or so I told myself. Okay, I cared, but it was only professional compassion, nothing more. Nothing to do with physical attraction. No way.

"We should see if they need help," I said. Technically, we should get as far away from here as quickly as possible, but if anyone needed my help, I'd stick around to give it.

"Keep near me," Zarex said.

That was the plan. I slipped my hand into his and we walked shoulder to shoulder.

A dozen steps and the laundry worker lay on the floor, presumably dead. Beside him, J'avet held his arm. His sleeve was torn, but I saw no blood.

"Blaster singe," he said with a grunt. "Security went after the last one."

More blaster shots and a shout sounded from a room nearby, followed by silence.

"I'll go check on that," Zarex said. "Edie, see to J'avet's arm." He trotted off before I could nod. So much for sticking close.

I frowned, but it wasn't as deep as the one on J'avet's face.

"I don't need help," he snapped.

"Let me look anyway," I said. "Medic's orders."

"That only goes for doctors." But he lowered his hand and let me get a good look. His skin was burnt as was the light fur around it, but it was shallow.

"You'll need to get that cleaned up and bandaged," I said, "but you'll live." Gently, I brushed away a corner of tattered fabric. When I did, my fingers touched his fur. A jolt of electricity passed through me, along with surprise at how soft he was.

"You're—"

He jerked away. "I'm fine, as you said," he growled. There was something in his eyes though, something which suggested he felt the jolt as much as I did.

I held my hands up in surrender and stepped away. "I'm going to see if Zarex is okay."

"You should stay here," he said. Before I might actually think he cared, he added, "You'll only get in the way and get him killed."

The second part was a good point, at least. I didn't want anything bad to happen to Zarex.

I nodded and looked away, but I was fuming. Partly because J'avet was such a jerk and partly because he was so confusing. He could be... Okay, maybe not nice, but something close to it. And then he could be a total ass a moment later. He changed so fast he gave me whiplash. Some part of me wanted him to whip me, but not like that.

I remembered what Zarex had said about the guys all giving me something different. J'avet gave me a challenge as much as he gave me a headache. Life was never dull with him around. He'd probably prefer to take a blaster shot to the head than be interested in me though.

"It's just us." Zarex's voice came out of the room before he did. He was followed by a haggard looking security officer. "And who knows how many nanobots who might search for a new home any moment now."

"We no longer need to go to engineering." J'avet gave me an accusing glance, which I ignored. "We should check the bridge." He accepted a blaster when Zarex handed him one.

Zarex nodded. "I can't guarantee that blaster is bot-free. Nor this one." He held up the weapon held in his hand. "But we might need them to save our asses. And Edie's." He offered me a warm smile.

I gave one back. "Does Edie get one?"

"You should return to the infirmary," J'avet grunted. "It's safer there."

"Safer, or out of the way?" I asked sweetly.

"Both," J'avet said coolly.

"We'll need her if anyone is injured," Zarex said in a tone which settled the matter. "Come on, we've spent enough time here."

J'avet turned on a heel, apparently done with us both, and started toward the bridge.

"Should we try to evacuate?" I asked.

Zarex looked rueful. "We could, but I can't guarantee we'd leave the Iri behind. None of the shuttles is equipped with a scanner. Not like the infirmary has at least."

I nodded. "Right, they aren't. I guess we're on our own to deal with this. Unless the IF decides to blow us up."

"Yes, unless that," he agreed. He looked rueful.

"Is…that likely?" I asked.

"If I was them, I would have lasered *Halcyon* to pieces by now," he admitted. "The threat to the IF is too great. What's a few hundred lives compared to that of every Freytaurian, or anyone the Iritauri might kill?"

"Not much, I suppose," I said. What a cheerful thought. "Still, it's my job to try to save lives until there are no other options. I prefer we do it that way first."

"Me too," Zarex agreed.

"Would you both shut up," J'avet growled over his shoulder. "You'll draw every nanobot on the ship to our location."

A rumble passed through the ship the moment he'd finished speaking, as though the words needed an exclamation mark.

"What the—" I said under my breath.

"Hurry," J'avet snapped.

I made a mental note to stay off ships once we reached Agus. If we ever did.

We reached the command area and J'avet pressed

the code to open the door. It slid open with almost ominous ease.

Slowly, and with eyes and ears open, we stepped inside. Nothing moved. Nothing made a sound except blood in my ears and the usual thrum of the engines.

I startled when the door whispered shut behind us, closing us in.

I had bad feelings before, but not like this. Fear crept up my skin like smoke.

When J'avet and Zarex moved forward slowly, I followed.

13

THE ONLY SOUND was my own breathing.

In.

Out.

In.

Out.

I concentrated on that to keep myself from imagining any number of things. We might have stepped into a room full of people going about their jobs as normal. The last time I was in here, it was quiet.

But... was it *this* quiet? I couldn't remember.

"The bridge is this way," J'avet whispered.

I barely heard the words, but his voice sounded loud.

I winced and nodded.

J'avet gestured for me to stay back and for Zarex to move forward with him.

Zarex nodded. He moved the blaster into his other hand. His face was drawn, brow creased in a deep frown. Worried, but not scared. Or scared, but hiding it well. He had probably faced worse than this before. What, I had no idea. I barely knew the man. When this was over, we'd have to sit down for a coffee and a nice chat. Did he even like coffee? That was another on a long list of things I wanted to find out.

I tiptoed after them, keeping what I hoped was a safe distance. I glanced into the rooms we passed, the few whose doors stood open. An administration room full of screens, another with a desk. A third held boxes piled on top of each other. Empty or full, I couldn't tell.

The corridor widened.

A shuffling sound came from somewhere up ahead.

We froze.

When no further sound came, we moved forward again. My whole body was so tense it almost hurt. Not in a good way. An orgasm wouldn't release this pressure.

"I smell blood," J'avet whispered.

My gaze swivelled to stare at him. What was he, a space vampire? That would explain why he was such a broody asshole. Luckily, only his eyes shone and not the rest of him. Well, he could stay the fuck away from my blood. My neck on the other hand...

Focus, Edie.

I sniffed. I smelt it too. A good deal of it must be spilled for it to be that strong.

"It's not blood," Zarex said. He seemed more troubled than ever. "It's the smell of acrolein."

J'avet and I both stared at him.

"Burnt fat," Zarex said. "It's the smell of bodies after—"

"Multiple blaster shots," J'avet finished.

"We should see if anyone is alive in there," I said uneasily.

Zarex nodded. His back straight, he marched toward the bridge. J'avet hurried to follow. Both men still moved with caution, but now with a new need to hurry.

I bit my lip and followed, but the smell became more pungent the closer we got. Burning flesh would have been more sickening, but this was bad enough.

We rounded a corner and I gasped out loud at the scene in front of me.

Three Iri lay dead. At least, I presume they were Iritauri. Hints of silver remained around their foreheads and on their lips. The rest of their skin was blue or purple.

The remainder of the bridge crew lay dead, slumped over consoles, or splayed on the floor. Most displayed blaster wounds, but one looked to have fallen or been pushed and hit their head hard enough to leave a fatal gash.

There was blood, but only smears here and there.

"They're all dead," Zarex said, his expression horrified.

"Who's flying this thing?" I asked softly.

J'avet's eyes widened. He hurried to a console and looked down at what looked like random letters and numbers to me.

"We're off course." He rubbed his forehead. "Headed for… Out of IF space."

"Can you put it back on course?" I asked.

He tapped a few buttons. "I'm locked out. We'd need a pilot with the right access, or the Captain." He waved toward a Centauri man on the floor. "The first officer is dead. They must have forced him to lock us out before they killed him."

"So the Iri are pirates now," I concluded. Fucking wonderful.

"We'll stop them," Zarex said. "We just need to get Brinley up here."

"Piece of cake," I muttered. "What if she's locked out too?"

"We'll cross that bridge when we get to it," Zarex said.

"I see what you did there," I said without smiling.

He looked wry and nodded. "I thought you might."

"Shhh," J'avet said.

I opened my mouth to tell him there was no one here to hear us, when I heard it.

Footsteps.

"Should we hide?" I hissed.

Zarex nodded. "Get down behind the console." He all but shoved me in that direction.

I ducked down and crouched, hands on the console a bare centimetre from its last operator. I sent them a silent apology for the disrespect of hiding near their dead body. I'm sure they wouldn't want us to end up the same way.

I squashed myself down as small as I could, while Zarex and J'avet hid behind their own consoles.

The footsteps drew closer.

I peeked around the side of the console and caught sight of a blaster. I wasn't sure if it belonged to the bridge crew or the Iri, but neither needed it now.

Without thinking, I darted out from my hiding place, grabbed the blaster and darted back before J'avet could do more than growl in annoyance.

Fuck him. Did he even care anyway?

I'd seen enough blasters to know which way to hold it, and where to press to fire it. At least I wouldn't shoot myself in the foot. Maybe.

The footsteps entered the room and stopped. They moved slowly toward the console, then moved away.

A voice swore.

"This is some fucked up shit."

I blinked.

Slek?

I was sure it was him, but I still moved slowly, peering out, blaster in hand, aimed at him. I caught sight of his hand. He too, held a blaster, ready to use.

"Who's there?" he called out.

I crab walked a step or two, looking carefully at the skin on his hand.

Finally, I sucked in a breath and rose.

The purple of his skin was the most beautiful thing I had ever seen.

"Hey," I said.

He turned suddenly and aimed at me. He lowered the blaster when he realised who he was aiming at.

"Edie, you're all right." He sagged with relief. "Um…"

"Oh." I lowered the blaster and hurried to embrace him. "Sorry. What are you doing here?"

"I could ask you the same thing." He raised an eyebrow as Zarex and J'avet stepped out from behind their hiding spot. "Just a wild guess, you weren't having a quickie back there?"

J'avet snorted.

Zarex managed a faint smile. "Not today, no. Can you unlock the controls? Hack the computer or something?"

"I can try," Slek said. "I have a reasonably high level of clearance, but not like the Captain or chief engineer, and they're both dead." He rubbed the back of his neck.

"This is starting to look like a coordinated effort," J'avet said. "There must be someone on board controlling all of this."

"Or close by," Zarex agreed. "Slek, have you got any idea of the range the nanobots can go and still receive orders or changes in their programming?"

Slek shook his head. "I would suggest a few thousand kilometres, but I'm guessing. Signals can extend a lot further, but whatever reaches them would be more complex than a simple hello, or cat video."

He gently moved a Garvi woman aside and knelt in front of her controls.

"Could we cut them off from whoever is sending the signal?" I asked. Okay, I'd probably watched too many episodes of *Star Trek*.

To my surprise, they all looked at me, mouths slightly open.

"We might," Slek replied. "But it depends where the signal is coming from." He scratched his head and looked conflicted.

"Keep trying to unlock the controls," Zarex said. "I'll see if I can hunt down the signal." He gestured for J'avet to help him move an Agusian from his chair. The man's antennae drooped like a dead plant. Zarex's drooped almost as much, in sympathy and sorrow.

They set the man to one side on the floor and Zarex slipped into his seat. He started to tap on the controls.

"I guess we'll keep watch," I said to J'avet.

He gave me a curt nod and turned toward the entrance.

I did the same, but kept the blaster by my side. If I tried to use it, I might end up hurting more than myself. Could blaster...well, blasts bounce off the walls? If so, I might kill one of the guys by accident.

Something caught my eye and looked toward the floor.

"Um, J'avet..."

"What?" he snapped. He realised what I was referring too and took a step back. He raised his blaster and shot at the swarm of nanobots which crept across the floor like an army of ants.

The blast singed the floor and blew a hole in the middle of the swarm. They closed over the breach, but there did seem to be fewer of them.

"Edie," he growled. He fired again.

"What if I hurt you?" I asked.

"Then I get hurt. I'm sure you won't cry over me," he snapped.

"I would," I replied. "I'm nice like that." I ignored his snort and aimed away from his feet. The recoil from the blaster was less than I expected. My shot also left a black scar across the floor, but fewer nanobots.

I aimed again, this time at a smaller cluster away from the rest. If I could take them out, they couldn't reform with the swarm.

Over and over again we fired, reducing the numbers even as they sought out metal to increase their numbers. It was a bit like shooting water in a drizzle. Now, there would be fewer, now more. The side of one of the consoles looked like it was chewed, or rusting quickly.

"Shoot faster," J'avet ground out.

"I'm trying," I replied. "Hey!" He shot so close to one of my feet, I had to jump sideways. A sting of pain shot through three of my toes.

"Sorry," J'avet said. "Move over further." I had barely stepped before he shot again. At least he missed me this time. Just.

I aimed and shot again and again. "My blaster is running out of juice." Each blast was weaker than the last.

"Here." Zarex tossed me his.

I almost dropped mine, but managed to catch his and throw mine to him. No sense in leaving metal around on the floor.

I pivoted with all the elegance of a brick and got off another couple of shots.

"That's almost all of them," J'avet said. He shot the console itself, holding down the trigger so the blast lasted for a minute, two minutes.

The smell of burning made me wrinkle my nose.

Finally he released the trigger and lowered the blaster.

"There's probably more, but unless they swarm like that again, we won't see them," he said.

I nodded and hoped like hells we could keep them from Slek.

"Any luck on the unlocking?" I asked.

He shook his head slowly. "I think this might be way above my pay grade."

"I've almost traced the signal," Zarex said. "It's close, very close, but I can't quite pin it down yet. I'll keep trying."

I ran a hand over my hair. It was probably as wild as ever, and then some. When this was over, I might have it all cut off. Crew cut like the guys. I would look silly, but at least it would be tame.

"You won't unlock the controls," a new voice said. "This ship belongs to the Iritauri now."

I turned and took on the sheen of silver skin, the set of now silver eyes, the blaster held in a silver hand.

My heart came to a grinding halt and I felt sick to my stomach.

"Danec?"

14

Danec smiled. "You missed one."

"So I see," I said. I surprised myself with how calm I sounded. On the inside, I was a trembling, quivering mess. The shape of his face and body were the same, but everything else was different. The way he held himself, the way he looked at me. He seemed curious, but the warmth was gone. The familiarity was gone.

No, not gone entirely; suppressed. He was still in there somewhere, I was certain of it.

"Can I ask where it hid?" I tried to see what J'avet and Slek were doing, but both were outside my peripheral vision.

Zarex hadn't moved from the console. Nor had he stopped tapping at it.

"Inside a tooth," Danec said. "Quite clever, don't you think?"

"Right." I had scanned his face. Somehow I missed that one, tiny speck of nanobot. Evidently that was all it took.

"I'm sorry."

He cocked his head in that adorable way he had. It was so... Danec, it hurt my heart.

"Danec wouldn't want this," I said. "Being a nanobot host wasn't on his bucket list."

He looked confused for a moment, then smiled. "Bucket list. List of activities to undertake before the body becomes deceased."

"Something like that, yeah." I felt the weight of the blaster in my hand. Could I use it on him? I wasn't certain I could.

"Don't be concerned," Danec said. "I'm still me, just enhanced. I have the knowledge of the Iritauri in my mind. It's like a vast library." He looked awed.

"That sounds, um, great," I said without a hint of enthusiasm. "But you don't have free will. You have to do what the nanobots say."

He blinked several times. "The relationship is symbiotic."

"Or parasitic," I muttered. "What will you do if they want you to kill me?"

"We have no desire to kill," he said.

I gestured around at all the dead bodies on the ship's bridge. "Excuse me if I find that hard to believe."

He looked toward the bodies closest to him. He seemed confused, as though the nanobots and Danec were in disagreement.

Good, keep fighting, I thought. *Fight them off.*

His head snapped up. "Only those who try to stop us will die," he said in a robotic tone. It seemed the bots won that round. "We wish no harm to the rest."

"Stop you from doing what?" I asked carefully.

Danec hesitated. "Joining the others. Making the Freytauri hosts. Modifying our programming so we're compatible with all other species."

"So, galactic domination," I said. "I don't think the IF will like that."

"The IF will be Iritauri in time," Danec said.

"You seem sure of that," I said.

"We have waited for this for a long time." He glanced around the bridge now. "Slek, you will be a host."

"I don't think so," Slek said from somewhere behind me. "I like my independence, but thanks anyway."

"You will be a host, or you will die," Danec said.

Slek stepped into my line of sight. "Back on Calig, we established that I'd rather die than be a host." He rubbed his chin. "In fact, we established that you felt the same way. I'm a really big fan of consent, and I don't think you've given it."

"Consent is irrelevant," Danec replied.

"Bullshit," Slek snapped. "Consent is everything. Danec knows that."

Danec looked confused, but shook his head. "I am Iritauri now. This is my purpose."

"A slave to the bots," Slek said. "Or whoever is controlling them. Who is that, by the way?"

I saw what he was trying to do; throw Danec off enough to reveal the origin of the nanobots, and maybe a way to stop them.

Danec paused, frozen like a computer awaiting input.

"You will all go to the mess," he said finally. "Those left alive will gather there."

"Why?" J'avet asked.

I had all but forgotten he was there.

Danec's head snapped to look at him. "That is the order. You will comply."

"Very well then," J'avet said. "Lead the way."

"No," Danec said. "You will lead. Place your blasters on the floor and move to the door." His blaster was aimed squarely at J'avet. He would use it, I had no doubt of that. The Iri had evidently established enough control over the ship they didn't feel the need to fight further unless forced to.

"Danec," I said carefully, "is Brinley okay? And Doctor Mazic?"

"Brinley is unharmed," he said, again speaking in that robotic voice. "Doctor Mazic is deceased."

I gasped. "What?"

"She tried to stop me." Was that a hint of regret in his eyes? If it was, it was a sign the real Danec was still in there. I had no idea how we'd get him back, but we had to try.

J'avet stepped past him and crouched to place his blaster on the floor at Danec's feet. He kept his eyes on the ensign the entire time.

When he rose, I let out a soft breath. I had half expected him to shoot at Danec. He was outnumbered and technically the enemy now. On the other hand, killing him might bring a bunch of Iri who would kill us. Cooperation might be the safer option right now.

Slek followed, but kept a distance from Danec. He looked nervous and confused.

I could relate to that. I wasn't sure why he hadn't

been inundated by nanobots by now. Presumably they figured they had plenty of time.

Rather than crouch, Slek tossed his blaster onto the floor and hurried after J'avet.

"Ladies first," Zarex said. He placed a hand lightly on the back of my neck.

"Thanks," I said ironically, but I was happy to have him at my back. Well, as happy as someone who was a prisoner of the Iritauri again could be. This was a habit I really would have preferred we not get into.

"It'll be all right," Zarex said softly.

I glanced over my shoulder, sure he referred to something in particular.

"I hope so," I said. The longer this went on, the more sure I was the IF would laser the *Halcyon* out of existence. Maybe I wouldn't blame them.

I added my blaster to the pile and moved to stand beside Slek. He slid his hand into mine and Zarex took the other.

Danec gave us a look. Was he jealous? Did he still think we could be together, nanobots and all?

I honestly couldn't guess what he was thinking. I wasn't sure I wanted to. I loved him, but how much of him was in there? I couldn't pretend things weren't different now. They were. Totally fucked up, and totally different. This wasn't how I anticipated my day going when I woke up this morning.

He shook his head as though dislodging a thought. "Walk," he said curtly.

"I see you've been taking diplomacy lessons from J'avet," I said lightly.

J'avet frowned at me, but said nothing.

"Too many words waste time," Danec said.

"I disagree," I said. "A good conversation is a way to get to know someone better. You want that, right? If we're all going to be Iri some day, then we might as well get along."

"The Iritauri are of one mind," Danec said.

"That's what I was afraid of," I said under my breath. "Do you mean that literally?" I asked.

"It must be difficult to control all those seperate hosts," Slek said. He looked thoughtful. "I mean, they aren't really one mind, or they would all be here, trying to make me one of them."

"Should you be reminding him?" I asked.

Slek glanced at Danec. "I have a feeling something else is going on here."

"Something bad?" I asked. My stomach fluttered with anxiety.

"Absolutely, without a doubt," he replied. "Very bad." He smiled, but the expression in his eyes spoke volumes about his fear. Every so often, he'd glance at Danec. They were like brothers, or friends. Now, I could almost put my hand on the tension between them.

The idea they might be enemies now made me want to build a blanket fort and hide inside with a teddy bear. I had no teddy, but I was sure I could find one, or something similar.

That brought my mind back to Brinley. I hoped Danec was honest when he said she was okay. I also hoped he lied about Doctor Mazic. The Danec I knew and loved would be horrified at the idea of killing anyone.

Or would he?

I reminded myself that he joined GASP. Would he join the military if he didn't expect to kill someone at some point? The logic made sense, but I still couldn't imagine Danec harming a soul.

This Danec might not have a choice.

He followed us to the mess and waved us inside.

"Is this all that's left?" I gaped.

From a crew and passengers of nearly two thousand, less than a hundred remained. The Iri numbered maybe fifty.

Slek was the only Freytauri left who hadn't been claimed as a host.

"Edie." Brinley half rose before she was waved back down again. "You're okay."

"So are you." I flopped down beside her before Danec or anyone could tell me not to. I gave her a brief hug and told her everything.

"I thought I would die," Brinley whispered. "One minute, Danec told us all our lives were forfeit. The next he told us to come here." She averted her eyes.

"Doctor Mazic refused."

"He really—" I swallowed a ball of regret.

"He shot her when she touched the comm panel. She tried to call for help." A tear slid down Brinley's cheek.

"It's not really him," I said firmly.

"It's him now," J'avet said.

I turned to glare at him. "He's—"

"He's Iritauri. Unless you have some way to change that, then you need to accept it. If you can't, you'll endanger us all."

I opened my mouth to retort, but closed it again. Fuck him, he was right.

"Fine," I said after a minute. "What do we do?"

"I found the signal," Zarex said softly. "It's coming from outside *Halcyon*, maybe from a nearby planet, but it's being relayed through the communications systems."

"If we can cut it, we might at least disconnect them from whoever is issuing orders," Slek said.

Zarex gave him a small nod. "If one of us is good with computers, they might even reprogram the nanobots." He looked meaningfully at Slek.

"I could do that, but we need to get out of here," Slek said.

"We'll need to create a distraction," J'avet said. "Something that might keep them busy for a while."

Slek rubbed his chin. "I wish I knew how much control Danec has. If I was Iri, I could—"

"No," I snapped. Sooner or later they would try, but for now I wouldn't let him sacrifice himself. If he was lost, we were screwed anyway. "I could try to *distract* Danec." I cleared my throat loudly.

"I'm sure seducing him would work on him, but that won't distract the rest of them," J'avet said dryly. "Unless you plan on distracting them all at once."

I smirked. "I'll do the men, you do the women." I said sarcastically.

"If I thought it would work, I'd do it," J'avet said. "But it won't. There are too many to keep focused all at once.

I pictured J'avet all hands, mouth and cock with a dozen Iri women and shook my head to clear the image from my head. "Do you have a better idea?" I asked.

"Not yet," he admitted. "Unless someone has an explosive in their pocket?" He looked around while we all said we didn't.

"I should have thought to carry around a bomb," I muttered.

"It was an oversight on all our parts," Slek said with a smile.

I snorted and jerked as Danec and two other Iri approached.

"Edie, Slek, come with us."

"In front of everyone?" I said sweetly.

Danec actually blushed. His face turned a darker silver and he averted his eyes.

There you are, I thought. *You're still in there.*

"This way," he said coolly. His expression was robotic again.

I sighed to myself, clasped Slek's hand and followed.

15

DANEC LED us to the galley, of all places.

"Oh good, I was feeling hungry," Slek said cheerfully. "I'd love a sandwich or two." He caught my expression. "What? A guy like me has a big appetite. I could eat two sandwiches as a snack."

"I believe it," I said. I couldn't even think about food right now.

"Food will be supplied at meal time," Danec said.

I forgot the Iri ate like everyone else. Of course they did, their bodies were organic. It was only their parasites which weren't. I presumed sooner or later they would also need to pee.

"I could handle a cup of coffee or two," I said. "Danec, have you introduced the others to the joys of coffee yet?"

I thought he might answer, but another Iri grabbed my arm and pushed up my sleeve.

"Hey." I almost jerked it back, but stopped myself at the last moment. Whatever they wanted, it was best not to anger them.

"Keep still."

I recognised the woman as another nurse. I wasn't sure if that was reassuring or not.

She grabbed out a needle from a box on the bench and pressed it into my vein. She drew out enough blood for a vial, then another and finally a third.

"Leave me some," I said under my breath.

She pulled the needle free and handed me a small bandage to stem the flow of blood. Her bedside manner could use some work.

I pressed the bandage to the small needle wound and tried not to object when they took blood from Slek as well.

"Keep him Freytauri," the nurse said, her expression and tone stone cold clinical. "We'll need him to provide blood for testing."

"Testing what?" I asked. I directed the question to Danec.

He hesitated like he was asking for orders and awaiting a response.

"Testing the impact of human blood on nanobots," he said finally. "When we know why it makes them dormant, we can stop it and humans can become hosts."

I shuddered. "And Slek's blood is for comparison?" I guessed.

Again, Danec hesitated. "Yes," he said after a minute.

"Good to know." Slek rubbed his arm. "I'm happy to let you borrow as much blood as you need."

Anything to keep him from becoming a host.

"So, about that sandwich," Slek said, as though that was the only thing on his mind at the moment. "I might pass out if I don't eat, after giving all that blood."

The nurse nodded and carried six vials out of the mess. Presumably the infirmary was their lab now.

"You may eat," Danec said. He opened a fridge and gestured toward a tray of sandwiches which the cooks presumably made before they died.

The idea made me both sad and sick, but we needed to eat, or we'd end up the same way. Hunger and my smart mouth didn't go so well together.

I grabbed up a couple of synthcheese sandwiches. "About that coffee…"

"You can return to the mess and sit down," Danec said.

"But…coffee." I sighed. "What about some water at least? Or juice. Or something. I'm thirsty."

"I'll find something. Go and sit." Danec looked torn between taking care of me, and the limit of the nanobot's programming. I assume they were only programmed for a limited amount of tolerance. I could relate to that, so was I.

"Fine." I gave him a long look, then took my sandwiches and walked back to the mess, Slek right behind me with three sandwiches.

"Here." I sat beside Zarex and handed him a sandwich. I gave Slek a meaningful look before he bit into one of his.

"But—" He sighed and handed a sandwich each to Brinley and J'avet. "I would have eaten all of those."

"I'm sure you would, but we need them alive too," I said as soothingly as I could manage, in spite of my jangled nerves.

J'avet looked at me over his bread as if he thought I would make a snide comment about not needing him alive.

For once, I said nothing. I wasn't in the mood to be that petty, even as a joke. We had to rely on each other now, like it or not.

"Thank you," Zarex said.

I nodded and told him why Slek was still Freytauri.

"Good, that will buy us some time," Zarex said.

"I wish we knew how long," I said. "They must have studied nanobots for decades. They might find the answer in a matter of hours."

"Or not at all," Slek said. "You humans are pretty complicated."

"You think so?" I asked.

"Absolutely," he said firmly. "Right Zarex?"

"Definitely," Zarex agreed.

"We really are," Brinley said, "but you guys are, too."

"You'll make me blush." Slek patted his cheek.

I smiled. "Now we're full of brain food, we need a plan." Personally, even after eating, my mind was blank. No, that wasn't true, but the ideas I had were bad ones, that would result is someone's death, if not that of all of us.

"How long until the IF gets here?" J'avet asked softly.

I looked at him in surprise. His eyes were fixed firmly on Zarex.

"It's been an hour since I sent the message," Zarex said. "It depends what other ships are in the vicinity, but I'd estimate another hour. Maybe two."

I frowned. "When you were looking for the Iri signal…"

"I sent a message to the IF, outlining the situation," Zarex said. "And the solution."

I sat back. "So we have an hour or two to find a way out, before they come and blow us all up?"

"Precisely," J'avet said.

I swung my face around toward him and asked, "How did you know?"

He shrugged. "It's what I would have done. Sometimes leading means making the tough decisions."

I wanted to retort, to yell and shout at them both. In the end, I just sagged. They were right. There may be no other option.

"Then we better work fast," Brinley said. "What if I distract them somehow and you all run off and do what you need to do?"

"They would notice four of us running off," J'avet pointed out. "And we don't need us all for this, just Slek."

Slek drew himself up and puffed out his chest. "It's nice to be appreciated," he said.

I smiled and patted his insanely big biceps.

"You're very appreciated. You're also very noticeable, being a big purple dude and all."

He exhaled as though deflated slightly. "I used to like being noticeable," he said sadly.

"It's a good thing," I assured him. "Just not when sneaking."

"Could we try to talk Danec into helping us?" Brinley asked.

"If I thought it would work, we could try," I said, "but I don't think it will. There's some of him left, but the bots are in control most of the time."

"Could we trick them?" Brinley asked.

Slek looked thoughtful. "I have an idea." He stood and waved his hands over his head. "Hey, I need to pee."

Several Iri looked his way and cocked their heads.

"I don't want to pee on the floor." Slek grabbed his groin. "Come on, guys."

Finally, one of the Iri nodded and waved his blaster toward the toilets off to one side of the mess.

"Do your business," he said. "Take no more than three minutes."

"Lucky I don't need to shit," Slek said. He stepped around me and hurried to the toilet.

"I guess he does his best thinking while he pees," I

said with a shrug. Fair enough. I do mine in the shower, or while half asleep. Exactly the wrong times to write anything down, but that was my brain for you.

I jumped a moment later when the ship's alarm sounded through the mess hall.

A voice came over the speaker.

"*Halcyon*. This is Commander Calderr of the IF vessel *Retribution*. All Iritauri will stand down and surrender all remaining crew, or you will be destroyed. You have five minutes to release escape pods. All Iritauri lives are henceforth forfeit."

My eyes widened. That was harsh. Was the IF not even going to attempt to save the Freytauri from the nanobots? I suppose not. Total destruction would be…well, easier. Awful, but simple and final.

The Iri gathered together in a cluster of confusion.

"Come on," Zarex pulled me to my feet and tugged me toward the door.

"Can we get to the pods in time?" I asked.

He shot me a smile over his shoulder. "We're not going to the pods."

I stared at him for a moment before I asked, "How—"

"Comm panel in the toilet and hacking skills." He shrugged.

The ship-wide alarm was deafening, but we made it to the door and into the corridor while the Iritauri milled about in confusion. It wouldn't take them long to figure out no other ship was out there.

We ran.

"Where are we going?" I panted.

"Comms," Zarex said. "We can shut ourselves in there."

Comms was just outside the command area. It felt as though it took us days to reach it, but it was only a handful of minutes. The corridor was empty except for the sound of the alarm and some Iritauri responding to the message.

"The Iritauri are all dead. It's safe to board."

Right, like anyone would buy that anyway.

"In here."

We darted into the darkened comms room. Slek skidded in behind us before J'avet closed the door.

"They're in chaos," he said gleefully. "They're trying to find a ship that isn't there."

"It is there," J'avet said. "Just not as close as they think."

"They may think it's a hoax when they really

arrive," I said. I wasn't sure if that was a good thing or not.

"In the meantime, hack away." Zarex waved at the computer screens. "I'm going to keep trying to find their signal *Halcyon*."

"I'll toy with the ship's internal sensors," J'avet said. "If I can, I'll have them fool the Iri into thinking we're somewhere else."

Zarex nodded. "Good idea."

"Can we remote control a pod?" I asked.

Zarex glanced at me, eyebrows raised. "Brinley?"

"I can try," she said. She slipped into a chair. "One escape pod with five life signs, coming up."

"I'll, um, watch the door," I said. I had no other particular skills to add.

"Edie." Slek waved toward another screen. "Can you access the medical database from here?"

"I would think so," I replied.

"Good. Access that and see what information they add after they've analysed our blood. Unless they send the information directly to the mother bot, then it'll be in there."

It's possible," I said doubtfully. If nothing else, I could see what Mazic had added, if she'd had time before Danec... I was glad to be seated in a corner, so no one could see the tears which trickled down my cheeks. Part of me wondered if all of this was to keep us all busy while we waited to die. We could spend our last hours telling jokes, or talking about our lives and deepest fears.

The other part of me had to believe we would get out of here alive. If I didn't hold onto that, I might give in to despair instead. That would help no one one.

Still, a small voice in the back of my head wondered if Danec was lost to me, even if I did make it out of this.

I bit back a sob and focused on the screen.

"They've tested the nanobots in every kind of blood," I said. They had been busy, but they didn't have answers.

Yet.

16

"THIS COULD BE A PROBLEM," Brinley said.

"What is?" Zarex asked.

"The ship has increased speed. I think they must know by now there's not another ship out there." Brinley toyed with her ponytail, but her eyes never left the screen.

"They probably suspect one is coming," Zarex said.

"I think I might have tweaked the scanners to show Iri as life signs," J'avet said.

"You think?" Zarex echoed. "I'd feel better if you were sure."

"Yes, I *think*," J'avet said. "It's not foolproof, but it's picking up clusters of nanobots. The good news is, if it's picking them all up, they're centred in the mess and galley."

"What's the bed news?" Zarex asked.

"The bad news is, it might not be picking them all up," J'avet replied.

"I prefer to assume they are," Slek said.

"There!" Brinley spoke suddenly. "One pod away. They may not buy that we're on it, but—"

"A dozen clusters of bots are moving away from the mess, toward the pod bay," J'avet said. "They must think there are others down there."

"Are there?" I asked.

"As far as I can tell, only a few others made a run for it when we did," J'avet said. "They're scattered around the ship. I can't tell them to come here without drawing attention to our presence."

I sighed and nodded. We would be more help to them if we stayed hidden.

"As it is, I have our position blocked, so anyone searching will find an empty room," J'avet added.

That was good to know. My friends and lovers were all so smart. I couldn't help but be impressed.

"There, I've found it," Zarex said.

"A human woman's G spot?" Slek asked. He gave me a smug look over his shoulder.

I flashed him a smile and had to force my eyes back to the screen. I would much rather he was exploring my body than sitting here trying not to die.

"Oh, I know where to find one of those," Zarex said lightly. "I found the source of the Iritauri signal. It's on a planet not far from here—Tarathu."

"Give me the coordinates," Slek said. "I think I can cut the ones on board off from that signal." He scratched his head. "We need to do more than that though."

"Can you take control of them?" Zarex asked. He tapped the coordinates for Tarathu into a tablet and handed it to Slek.

"I— Maybe. I'll need more time." Slek leaned over the screen, his nose almost touching the glass.

"That's strange," Brinley said. "Another pod left the pod bay."

"Who's on board?" Zarex asked.

It was J'avet who responded. "Six clusters of nanobots."

"Six Iritauri," I said softly. "Are they going after the other pod?"

"They're going in the same direction, yes," Brinley said.

"Shit," Slek muttered. "I can't cut them off if they're not on board. Or take control of them."

"Focus on the others," Zarex said. He sat back and cracked his hands over his head.

Slek nodded. "I'm going to try to cut them off, then take control. If I'm too slow, they may react badly."

"By react badly, you mean…" I ventured.

"Kill the non-Iri on board," Slek said.

"Ah. That would suck," I agreed. And hard. If anyone died because of what we did, that would be difficult to live with. Assuming we lived much longer. Which I was assuming, because I wasn't nearly ready to die yet. Not even close. Nope.

"Yes, it would suck, and not in a good way," Slek said. "Ready—"

He was cut off by a banging on the door.

"Open up," a voice ordered. "We have your fellow crewmen here. For every minute you delay, one dies."

I glanced at J'avet, who cursed under his breath.

"They masked their presence," he growled. "There's five Iri and ten crew or passengers out there."

"Slek, now would be the time," Zarex said.

Slek shook his head. "I need to get a fix on them all first. Give me two minutes."

"We might not have two minutes," Zarex said.

"I'll open the door," I said. "I'll try to buy us some time while you do your magic."

"This is nowhere near my magic," Slek said without looking away from the screen. "When this is over, I'll remind you of that."

"You'd better," I replied. I hopped up from my chair and hurried across to the door controls.

"Don't shoot," I shouted. "I'm coming out."

I tapped the button by the door and stood back, arms crossed over my chest.

As J'avet said, fifteen sets of eyes looked right at me. Several Iri had blasters to the heads of a variety of species: a Garvi man, a Centauri woman, a young Agusian and and a human whose sex I couldn't tell by looking. They looked the most scared of all.

"Hi." I put my hands out to either side and smiled. "That's quite the welcoming committee for little old me." I tucked a few strands of hair behind my ear and batted my eyelashes sweetly.

"Step out of the room," one of the Iri ordered. Her skin was such a pale silver, I suspected she was a light purple to begin with. A lovely shade of lavender, no doubt. With any luck, she would be again. With even more luck, it would be soon. Like, any moment now. I resisted the urge to look back over my shoulder. I needed all of their attention to be on me right now.

I took a few steps, my eyes on Lavender. She seemed to be the leader of this group.

"There, I'm out," I said nicely. "No need for blasters, I'll come quietly. Or loudly if I ever get the chance to come agai—"

Lavender squeezed the trigger of the blaster and the young Agusian man died without a word, a shocked expression on his face.

"Hey, I said I would do as I'm told." I curled my hands into furious fists. My eyes burned with hot tears. What the absolute, everloving fuck? So much for not killing unless someone got in the way.

"That is for disobedience." Lavender placed her blaster into her other hand and slapped me hard across the face.

I reeled back, almost into the wall. My cheek stung. The urge to strike her back was so strong I literally bit my lips to keep from doing it.

"There's no need for that." That was J'avet, right behind me to catch me and keep me from falling and retaliating. "We'll comply."

That was apparently not enough for Lavender. She nodded to one of her companions, who slammed his blaster hard into J'avet's groin.

I expected the Parvoran to double over in pain.

I didn't expect the cracking sound the impact made. I certainly didn't expect to see the blaster with its nozzle bent, held in the confused Iri's hand.

J'avet looked entirely unimpressed, bored even. How was he not writhing in pain? He must have a cast iron dick, or something. Did he give new meaning to the expression 'boner'? As in literal bone?

Lavender growled. "Back to the mess. Any more insubordination and you die."

I arched my eyebrows at J'avet. "You're going to have to explain that to me at some point."

He just smiled. Actually smiled.

"Where are the others?" Lavender leaned to the side to peer into the comms room. She jerked, then froze.

"Got it," Slek declared. "I've told the nanobots to stop and await further orders."

"That is what it looks like, yes." J'avet eased the blaster out of Lavender's hand and nodded for the rest of the crew to do the same. "Assuming it was you who did it."

"If not him, then it's the biggest fucking coincidence in the history of the universe," I said. I might have exaggerated slightly, but it would be pretty big.

"What now?" Slek asked.

"Can you ask the nanobots to get the fuck out of them?" I asked.

"We'll need a place to put them," J'avet said.

"I can think of a place," I said. "Let's make it easier for the IF to destroy them."

"Um, speaking of them," Brinley said, "we have an incoming message."

"Put them through," J'avet and Zarex said at the same time.

J'avet gave Zarex his customary scowl, but turned back to keep an eye on Lavender.

"This is Pilot Brinley Grant, on board *Halcyon*. We, um, have the situation under control now."

The screen flickered and a Freytauri face appeared.

"This is Captain Yaranin of the *Chimera*. We received a curious distress signal from the *Halcyon*. Something about nanobots and destroying the ship with a laser." He looked amused and I was reminded of Slek, but with Danec's skin colouring.

"False alarm," Zarex said. "In a manner of speaking. As Pilot Brinley said, we have the situation somewhat under control. There's the small matter of some nanobots."

"Commander Zarex, it's good to see you," Yaranin said. "You're not usually given to exaggeration."

Zarex ran a hand over his forehead and up to the top of one antenna. "You and a security team should come over here. I'll explain everything and we can discuss what to do next."

"Keep an eye out for a pod or two," Slek said. "Shoot first, ask questions later."

"Noted." Yaranin looked at someone over his shoulder and nodded. "We'll be there within the hour."

"We'll keep a light on," Slek said.

Yaranin chuckled and the screen went blank.

"All right, let's try to take the nanobots out of her first." Zarex waved at Lavender. He pulled out a drawer and emptied the contents on the floor. "Make sure you tell them not to eat anything."

"Will do." Slek worked the controls in front of him and Lavender quivered.

"Gently," Zarex said.

"Moving gently," Slek confirmed.

Lavender shuddered and the silver leached from her face, bit by bit. It was slower than with Danec, but once it started, it became faster and faster. After thirty or forty seconds, her face was, as I suspected, lavender coloured. The silver faded from her hair and a cloud of darkness crept across the floor and into the drawer.

"That was so much easier than with Danec," I muttered. I moved to help J'avet grab Lavender and lower her to the ground. I felt her neck for a pulse and crouched beside her, my eyes focused in concentration.

"She's alive. Her pulse is a bit rapid, but steady. Physically, I think she'll be okay." Mentally, she'd probably need some therapy. We all would.

The rest of the nanobots started to leave the Freytauri. Another one was a dark purple and the other three were blue, like Danec. Strangely, one man's hair stayed silver around the edges.

"He might have been like that to start with," J'avet said.

"I suppose so," I said. It might also be from stress. I probably had a grey hair or two after this.

"We should go down to the mess and collect the bots from the people down there," I said. Especially Danec. My heart fluttered at the idea of seeing him again, totally bot-free. He, too, would need therapy, particularly to help him come to terms with what happened to Doctor Mazic. I couldn't bring myself to blame him for it. The parasites had done it, not him. He was just an innocent, unwilling host.

"Are you giving orders now?" J'avet snapped.

I sighed. "I don't understand you," I said. "Sometimes you're almost nice, then you're an asshole again. Can you make up your mind?"

He gave me a long, intense look that made my panties want to twist into a knot and combust. Or maybe that was my clit. Or both. Or—

"I wouldn't want anyone getting too familiar," he said finally. "They might get expectations."

I snorted. "Fine, keep everyone at arm's length. It's a lonely way to be." I was guessing, but it sounded about right.

"It's a safer way to be," he stated. He turned away before I could see his expression. "Let's head to the mess."

"Didn't I already say that?" I asked. I wasn't going to give him a centimetre of leeway. If he wanted to be a dick, then so be it.

He sighed and rose. Without a glance back, he strode away.

"We'll need to get everyone to the infirmary," I said to one of the security officers, who sat shaking her head and looking in confusion at her blue skin. "When you're ready," I added.

She nodded. "I'll see to it. Once everyone is… oriented again."

I put a hand on her shoulder. "It'll be okay now. We'll get rid of the bots and the IF will make sure they can't take control of any of you again." I knew I was making a promise the IF might not be able to keep, but she nodded and seemed comforted by the words.

"I have to go and see to the others." I rose and gave her a smile before I trotted off after J'avet. With his long legs, he was probably halfway there by now, but my desire to see Danec pushed me to trot just that much more quickly. More than anything, I wanted him back to himself before the crew of the *Chimera* arrived. I don't know why that was important, but it was. Maybe it was simply a matter of Danec's pride.

17

"WHERE IS HE?" I looked around the mess full of passengers and very still Iritauri. As far as I could tell, Slek's control held them, even as far from the comms room as we were.

"He can't be far." J'avet tapped the comm panel on the wall. "We're ready."

Slek's voice came through in response. "Okay, de-botting now."

As before, the nanobots slid down from their hosts and into boxes held by me and J'avet. The passengers and crew moved to catch the freed hosts before they hit the floor. Several crashed before anyone could reach them. There were simply too many at once.

I winced each time one hit the floor and

groaned. At least they were under their own control now, and broken bones mended easily enough.

"I don't see him," I said, half frantic with worry for Danec. "I'm going to check the galley." I closed my box and thrust it at J'avet, who managed to grab it before he dropped it.

I thought J'avet might argue, but I turned my back on him so I couldn't see him scowl. I didn't need his judgement right now.

I marched into the galley. "Danec?"

The place was empty except for half a tray of sandwiches which sat on the bench.

I left it there and stepped back out into the mess. Several Freytauri were sitting up now, rubbing aching heads and attempting to reorient themselves after what they'd been through. More than one looked completely confused. I wasn't sure if I hoped they remembered later what had happened, or if they were better off not knowing. Some had killed. That was something I imagine would be difficult to reconcile. I know if it was me, I would struggle with it.

I crouched beside one, a young woman in an ensign's uniform, like the one Danec wore.

"Hi," I said lightly. "Have you see Danec? Hot guy,

blue skin, great ass. He should be himself again by now."

She blinked at me a couple of times and shook her head. "I think he went with the others to the pod."

My heart sank. So they did remember. Wait—the pod? Admittedly, I was part of the way to thinking that might be the case, but even now I didn't want to accept it.

I smiled. "Are you sure?"

"I— no, but I… My memory is foggy. It was like being stuck behind a curtain. I could see out a little bit, but I couldn't pull it aside. I tried, but I just—" She dissolved into tears.

I put my arms around her and held her while she cried on my shoulder.

"It's okay," I said softly. "You're safe now. We have the bots under our control. You'll be fine." I rubbed her back gently until her sobs subsided.

Fine. It was easy for me to say that. She might never be okay. I felt a flash of anger toward the Iritauri and the nanobots. Did galactic domination have to be so ugly?

I drew in a breath through my nose. I was more determined than ever to do whatever I could to help ensure they failed at that objective.

Eventually, she pulled back and rubbed her eyes.

"Thank you. This is my first time away from Frey-T and..." She sniffed.

I patted her shoulder. "This is my first time away from Earth. It's been a lot more exciting than I expected." And terrifying. And horrible. And sexy. But also awful.

"Yes. Same here." She looked like she'd happily share a blanket fort and a bottle of wine with me sometime, but for now, I needed to find Danec.

"I'll talk to you later, okay?" I gave her a reassuring smile and rose. Careful to step around dazed Freytaurians, I walked over to where J'avet stood, peering into a box o' bots.

"She thinks he's on the pod," I said, my voice low.

J'avet nodded. "All right."

I did a double take. "All right?" I echoed. "Is that all you can say?"

He looked up at me and frowned. "What else would I say? If he's on that pod, he's out of our reach."

"He might be in reach of the *Chimera*," I said bitterly.

"Possibly. If that's the case, there's nothing we can do." He sounded so blasé, so calm I could only stare.

"What about we tell them what Slek did? Maybe they can do the same?"

"I'm sure Zarex has already done that." He snapped the lid of the box shut and handed it to one of the security officers. "See this gets to the isolation room in the infirmary and that no one enters the room or touches anything inside."

"Yes, sir," the officer said smartly.

J'avet turned to me. "Hysterics won't help the ensign or anyone else," he said coldly.

"It would help me," I said, my hands on my hips. "Or better yet, some casual stabbing."

He rolled his eyes. "You ask why I keep you at arm's length. This is why."

"Because I have feelings?" I demanded. "Because I dare to care about someone other than myself?"

He grabbed my arm and pulled me into the corridor and from there into a small room. I couldn't guess the purpose of it and, to be honest, I wasn't paying much attention. I was too busy being distracted by my desire to punch him in the face and my other desire to melt into a puddle on the floor.

"Do you realise where you are and *who* you are?" he growled.

I started to glance around, but he jerked me around to face him.

"You're on the *Halcyon*," he snapped. "You're one of the people who survived the Iritauri incursion. You helped to stop them. Further," he said before I could respond, "you're a medic. You're one of the people the other survivors will need more than anyone else. If you don't pull yourself together, you'll be no use to anyone, including yourself."

"Not that you care," I retorted.

He gave me a long, long look. For a while, I thought he would hit me or kiss me. My heart thudded so fast I thought it might burst out of my chest.

Then he stepped away. "Go and see to your patients. I'll send a few people to help clean the infirmary and give you what help you need. I'll be sure they know where Danec might be." he stepped toward the door. "He might also be dead."

Before I could even think well enough to swear at him, he was gone.

I slumped against the wall and trembled. He was right, but I hated that fact. I wanted to hate him, but I understood what he tried to do. It was my job to take care of the people left on the ship, especially the former hosts. I needed to focus on them, not myself.

By the time I stepped out of the room, there was no sign of J'avet. I ran my fingers through my hair and hurried off to the infirmary. I had to put my faith in Zarex, Slek and even the chance Danec would turn up in the infirmary. Deep down though, I knew the *Chimera* was armed with lasers and every reason to use them against the pod.

The infirmary was bustling when I stepped inside. To my relief, one of the doctors stood beside a bed, speaking to a young man with wide eyes and wet cheeks.

I half expected to see Mazic or even Kalvix, but both were gone. Both victims of the Iri and the rogue Freytauri who wanted the nanobots eradicated. In retrospect, the rogues had a good point. Perhaps we should have listened to them. They didn't give us the chance, but still…

Every so often, crew would enter, carrying bodies into the morgue. That would be full soon, if it wasn't already. I thought about looking for Danec, but before I could take a step, I spotted the young woman from the mess, and Brinley, who sat by her bed. They had their heads together and were talking in low voices.

Brinley laughed and the Freytauri woman smiled.

As I approached, Brinley looked up and grinned.

"Edie! This is Harva. I was just telling her how good chocolate is."

"It really is," I agreed. "I'll have to see if I can find you some." I could do with a block or two myself, and a bottle of vodka. Not necessarily in that order.

"I should look at your head," I said to Brinley.

"I feel fine," she replied.

I arched an eyebrow at her. "Are you going to be a difficult patient?"

"Would I dare?" she asked, rising to her feet.

"Without a doubt," I teased. "Come on, let me take a quick look."

"You can take a long look," a voice said in my ear.

I turned and threw myself into Slek's arms. I told him about Danec. He held me and rubbed my back while he listened.

"We know where they're going," he said. "The IF will send people after them."

"We're people," I pointed out.

"That we are," he agreed. "See to Brinley. The *Chimera* should be here within the hour."

I nodded. I wanted to be there when it did. I nodded to know if they'd seen the pod. If they'd...

I couldn't think about that. Danec had to be okay. Whatever happened, we'd find him and rid him of the parasites once and for all.

I waved Brinley over to a chair and checked her

head. There was no sign of fresh blood, but it would take time to fully heal.

"You should rest," I said finally.

"So should you." She put a hand on my arm. "We've all been through a lot."

"Danec most of all," I said.

"I almost became a host," Slek said as he flopped into the chair beside Brinley.

"Almost doesn't count," she told him.

He pretended to be offended. "Of course it does. They took my blood, the fiends."

Brinley smiled. "You must be traumatised."

"I am," he agreed.

I rolled my eyes. "I'm sure the rest of the Frey-tauri on board would suggest their trauma is worse than yours."

His smile faded and he gave me a rare, serious look. "I know," he said softly. "I wanted to—"

"Make me feel better?" I suggested. "I know, I just…" Tears prickled my eyes.

"We'll find him," Slek said firmly. "We'll save his sorry little ass and get him to Agus to finish his studies. Before you know it, he'll be a commander and as bossy as J'avet and Zarex."

"Nicer than J'avet, " I growled.

"With a better ass," Brinley added.

"Oh, I don't know, J'avet has a pretty hot ass," Slek said.

I grimaced. "Yeah. Shame he is one, too."

Slek chuckled. "Yes. He certainly keeps us all on our toes."

"Yeah." That reminded me. I told Slek about how one of the Iri had hit him hard in the groin, but all he'd achieved was to break the blaster.

"Pubic plate," Slek said.

"Come again?" I asked.

He grinned. "I'd love to." He wiggled his brows. "Parvoran men have a plate of bone over their genitals. It's like an eyelid, but hard, and over his cock."

I blinked and shook my head. "That sounds like quite the evolutionary advantage."

Slek cocked his head. "It really does, doesn't it? I'm jealous. I wonder if I could get one made." He scratched his head while I laughed softly.

"You could try staying out of trouble," I suggested.

"What would be the fun of that?" he asked, a twinkle in his eye.

The ship jolted and I froze. I pushed down the rising fear and listened to a metallic clang from somewhere else on the *Halcyon*.

For a moment I thought something else had gone wrong. Then I realised what I was hearing.

"It sounds like the *Chimera* has arrived," Slek said.

Heart in my throat, I followed him and Brinley out the door and toward the pod bay. Just let them try to keep us out. I had to find out what they knew about Danec and I had to know now.

"WE ATTEMPTED TO INTERCEPT THE POD," Yaranin said.

Getting in was easier than I anticipated. In fact, Zarex was waiting with an open door and outstretched hand. He drew me to his side while J'avet scowled.

Let him scowl, I thought. I drew myself up and put my professional face on. Whatever the captain had to say, I would listen and I wouldn't cry, scream or shout until I was well away from J'avet. He wouldn't see me lose control ever again.

"Attempted?" Zarex asked.

"We passed within communication distance," Yaranin said. "We had a brief conversation, but they cut and ran. They hid amongst a comet field. *Halcyon* was the priority. The IF will seek them out."

"Can we see that conversation?" Zarex asked. He gave me a sidelong look and reassuring smile. Which didn't reassure me, but I appreciated the effort.

Yaranin's eyebrows twitched, but he nodded. He glanced over to a commander behind him, who disappeared back into their pod.

"I'll have the message relayed to the screen in here." He eyed me speculatively, as though uncertain as to why I was there, but he said nothing.

A few moments later, the large screen on the wall snapped to life.

"This is the IF vessel *Chimera*." Yaranin's voice came over the speaker.

"Sir, there are no life signs," another voice said.

"Commander Zarex said to expect that," Yaranin said. "See if you can open communications anyway."

"Yes, sir."

The vision on the screen changed from black to the dimly lit interior of a pod. Two silver-skinned figures sat in the seats in the cockpit. Four more were arrayed behind them.

My heart stopped.

Danec stood on the right side of the screen, face blank. His glazed eyes stared straight ahead. If I didn't know this was a recording, I would think he was looking at me. Watching me. Trying to communicate with me.

A breath caught in my throat.

I found Slek's hand on my shoulder. I covered it with mine.

I only half listened to the conversation. Mostly I just felt sick. I should have tried to reach Danec when he was still onboard *Halcyon*. I could have talked to him, reasoned with him, or knocked him out cold and dragged his cute little ass with us. Anything. Instead, I'd run, looking after my cute little ass instead. I sucked. I swallowed down the need to vomit. I couldn't even take pleasure from imagining puking on J'avet's boots. All of that seemed so fucking petty right now.

I licked my lips and caught the end of the communication.

"We will not surrender. Iritauri will... all will be hosts..."

The screen flickered and went black.

"They've passed out of IF space, sir. Should we pursue?"

The message ended.

"Are you okay?" Slek whispered.

I shook my head. "I'll be okay when we get him back."

"Captain Yaranin," J'avet said, "the bridge is set up for a briefing."

Cleared of the bridge crew's bodies, you mean, I thought bitterly. He spoke like their lives had no meaning at all. Like they weren't even people. I wanted to punch him in the face. I wanted to punch myself more, for not doing enough. Okay, I don't know what more I could have done, that wouldn't have ended with me dead too, but that didn't take away from my current self loathing. Survivor's guilt. Whatever.

"Engineer Slek, can you brief the *Athena's* crew on the method you used to gain control of the nanobots?" J'avet asked.

Slek shot me a lopsided grimace, but turned and nodded. "Sure. It's a skill we're all going to need to have, until they're eradicated."

"I'll ensure those who need rest get it," Zarex said. "Including me." He stifled a yawn with his fist.

"I'll speak with you later," Yaranin said. He followed J'avet from the room, accompanied by his security team and Slek.

"I'm so sorry." Zarex faced me and cupped my face in his hands. He ran a thumb over my cheek.

"We'll find a way to keep him safe, I promise. You need him, so I need him. I need him to give you what I can't." He smiled slightly. "Besides, I like the guy."

"I like him too," I said softly. "The nanobots can't have him." I made what I hoped was a fierce face, but probably ended up as scary as a puppy.

Zarex smiled, but his eyes were laced with worry. "I meant what I said about getting some rest. Come on."

He wound an arm around my waist.

"Where are we going?" I asked.

"My cabin," he replied, a sly expression on his green face.

"Why do I think rest is the last thing on your mind?" I asked. Truthfully, it was the last thing on mine. His proximity and the memory of his mouth on my lips made my blood hot in spite of myself.

"It's the last thing I want to do," he replied. "After I do a lot of much more interesting things to you."

"Oh, like what?" I asked.

"I don't want to spoil the surprise."

I made a face. "I hate surprises. After the last few weeks, I'd like a bit of dull and boring in my life."

"I apologise for being neither of those," he said, but he smiled while he spoke.

I poked him in the chest. He was all hard muscle under my fingertip.

"You're right, you're not boring, but you are less of a rollercoaster than J'avet."

"Rollercoaster," Zarex repeated. "Old Earth fun park ride, right?"

"Yes," I agreed. "Too many ups and downs and then all you want to do afterward is be sick."

Zarex laughed. "That doesn't sound like fun."

"It doesn't, but it is." Maybe that was why I couldn't get J'avet off my mind, no matter how much of a dick he was.

He leaned in and whispered in my ear. "I'll show you a much more fun ride."

"Promises, promises," I replied. Yet the idea of him touching me everywhere was driving me wild. My skin tingled at the thought.

"How far is your cabin?" I asked. If it was any further, I might throw caution to the wind and tear his clothes off there and then in the corridor.

"Just around the bend," he said.

I half expected Iri to jump out at us, blasters in hand, but they didn't. The corridor was deserted and eerie. That was another in a long line of reasons I was relieved when he stopped in front of a door and pressed the button to open it.

Having never been in the cabin of anyone in command before, I was surprised to see it wasn't much bigger than the rest. The view was the same, of course; stars upon stars. The bed was a similar size, barely big enough for two to lie side by side. At least it wasn't a hammock.

His bed cover looked handmade and well loved. When he noticed me looking, he said, "My mother made it. I take it with me everywhere." He clapped a hand to his forehead. "That sounds pathetic."

I wound my arm around his neck. "It sounds sweet. And practical. And...like you love to have a piece of home with you. I have a small, plush bunny I keep hidden in my bag. It smells like the laundry powder my mother uses." When I felt homesick, I'd pull it out and take a long sniff.

He smiled softly, then drew me into his arms for a searing kiss.

I felt the tension in Zarek's touch and knew it wasn't just lust for him either. We both needed to let ourselves go for a while. Let our bodies do the talking, to give our mouths and minds a break. Truthfully, I wouldn't sleep now anyway, my thoughts were too heavy. A part of me kept guard for any news, but the rest surrendered to the here and now.

Zarex slipped his hands under my shirt and

pulled it off, almost without breaking off our kiss. Our lips were apart for all of about five seconds. Maybe six. Then another six while we both pulled off his shirt and tossed it aside.

Before I could take a breath, my bra was on the floor and Zarex lifted me and carried me over to the bed. He didn't even look as though he struggled. But then, he was almost as big as Slek in the muscle department. He probably lifted twice my weight before breakfast. And three times that afterward.

Zarek's mouth left mine and he kissed his way down to my breasts.

"Human women are so soft," he whispered.

"Compared to who?" I asked. My sisters from all the other species I'd met looked pretty soft too. I mean, I was no expert here, especially since I looked and didn't touch.

Zarex trailed the tip of his tongue over my nipple and smiled. "Compared to everything. Except those marshmallows they make on Earth."

"Right." I quivered under his touch. "Those are extremely soft."

"They aren't as sweet as you though." He trailed his tongue the other way. His antennas bent toward my face, as though watching for my reaction.

"They taste better in hot chocolate than I would,"

I said with a nod. I would just get hot, not melt into sticky gooeyness. Although, Zarex was doing a pretty good job getting me gooey.

Zarex chuckled. "I don't know about that. I'm not sure anything would taste better than you." He captured my nipple with his mouth and suckled gently.

"I'll take your word for it." I wasn't sure how I managed to get out the words. My thoughts weren't all that coherent.

He smiled and moved to the other nipple, while his hands shed my clothes from the waist down. Then his.

I lifted my head, trying to get a good look at his two cocks, but he moved down and buried his head between my legs. Man of mystery, I guess. Fine, I could be patient. For a little while.

My head flopped back and I closed my eyes as he lapped at my folds with firm, confident strokes.

I gripped handfuls of bedcovers in either fist and breathed out my nose as he licked and suckled on my clit. Every so often, he would slip the tip of his tongue inside me, and lick around my entrance.

I saw stars, nebulas, whole galaxies as he took me closer to coming. My breath came in little pants, like a series of moans getting higher and higher.

Finally I was swept away in a rush of sensation and fluid. One rushed into me, encompassing me like a warm sea of desire and pleasure. The other rushed out like a warm river of desire and pleasure. Ummm... Oops.

"Oh." Before I even fully came down, my eyes shot open. I lifted my head to see Zarex wipe his cheek with the back of his hand. "I'm sorry, I've never... That's never happened before." Oh gods, swallow me up now.

Instead of being horrified or grossed out, Zarex smiled. "I like to see how much I turned you on. Apparently it was a lot."

I mean, he wasn't wrong.

He scooted up the bed and lay beside me. Now I got a good look at those cocks. I was right, it was one at the base, but split just above. Individually, they looked thick enough for a bunch of fun.

"So, how does this work?" I asked.

"Like this." Zarek turned me on my side, facing him and hooked my leg over his. He guided one of his cocks to my entrance and slid it inside. The other bent like a tentacle and teased my clit.

"Okay, that works," I said.

Zarex smiled and thrust into me several times,

slowly and deliberately. Then he pulled his cock out all the way. It was shining, slick with my juices.

His eyes on mine, he manoeuvred so his other cock could slide into my entrance. He eased the tip of the wet cock into my rear hole.

"Then there's this," he said. Simultaneously, he slid a cock into each hole, slowly, carefully, watching for any sign of discomfort. "I have some natural lubricant of my own, but yours added a little something to smooth the journey."

"Oh my..." Holy shit, this felt amazing. It was like being with two guys at once, only...not. I had never felt so deliciously full before. It was incredible, amazing, arousing and a bunch of other superlatives I couldn't think of right now.

He drew back and thrust again. A groan slipped from his lips.

That drove me close to having another orgasm on the spot. I'd had guys in all my holes, but never more than one at a time. My ass and my pussy both wanted more.

I pushed my hips forward, driving him deeper, until it almost hurt.

He thrust harder, faster.

"Edie," he whispered. "I'm falling for you."

His words tugged me toward the edge so fast I could barely resist.

"I'm falling for you too," I said. I could certainly get used to this. He was different to the other guys. No one was better than another, but between them, I'd be satisfied. A lot. like, really a lot. If only they didn't expect me to choose at some point. Gods, I didn't want to think about that now.

Another thrust or two and I came again, this time without the squirting. If that was the new normal, I would have to get used to it, but not all at once.

Zarex grunted and his hips moved faster.

I felt both of his cocks become even stiffer as he groaned and ground hard into me. Warm heat flooded into my pussy and ass. Evidently both cocks came at once. Good to know.

He ground for a while longer, then sagged down beside me.

"Wow," he said breathlessly.

"Double wow," I said with a smile.

He chuckled and slid carefully out of me and drew me to him.

"You were everything I imagined, and more," he said softly.

"You too." I snuggled down to his chest. Even my

wild imagination couldn't have conjured him. Or any guy with two dicks, let's face it.

"You should sleep." He kissed the top of my head.

"You too," I said again. I was too tired to think up new words. I closed my eyes, exhaled softly and let sleep take me.

19

"Captain Yaranin will be taking command of the *Halcyon*," J'avet said. He didn't seem pleased to be saying those words.

I guessed he wanted the command for himself, but too bad. I looked around the briefing room. No one seemed surprised or disappointed, except J'avet himself. Yaranin seemed pleased, even smug. *Halcyon* was at least twice the size of the *Chimera*. To get her and such a small crew to the nearest port would be a challenge. The post would bring him prestige. Great if you're into that kind of thing. Me, I was happy to be alive.

J'avet—well, no wonder he was pissed.

His tone lightened, barely perceptibly. If

someone didn't know him, they'd miss it entirely. "I'll be taking command of the *Chimera*."

I blinked several times in surprise. A rumble of chatter passed through those in the room, but it died down when he glared.

"The *Chimera* is under orders to pursue the Iritauri."

That declaration was met with another ripple of surprised chatter.

"To that end," J'avet said over the noise, "Commander Zarex will accompany me, as will Engineer Slek."

Both guys looked as shocked about that as I was.

"The *Chimera's* current crew will stay aboard, apart from several security officers who will transfer to *Halcyon*. Those already on board *Halcyon* will remain and accompany the ship to port. From there, another ship will take you to your destination."

My lips dropped apart. I knew it was possible Zarex would be posted elsewhere, but it didn't think it would be *now*. And Slek—he was supposed to accompany me to Agus. It made sense for him to go after Danec and the others, but I wasn't ready to be parted from all of the guys, not yet.

I shook my head. "That's not—"

Slek put a hand on my knee and squeezed. "We'll talk to him. You should be included in this too."

"It's J'avet's call," Zarex said uncomfortably. "You would be safer away from all of this."

I looked at him through my eyebrows. "Excuse me? Have I not proven myself to be a badass?"

He shifted in his chair. "Of course you have. I just…"

I raised an eyebrow.

"I don't want you to get hurt."

"I don't want you to get hurt either," I said. "Slek is Freytauri and he's going."

"He has certain skills." Zarex's tongue flicked over his lips. He wasn't going to win this argument and he knew it.

"I have skills," I argued. "What if you get injured?"

"The *Chimera* has medics," Zarex pointed out. "Experienced ones. And *Halcyon* has a lot of people who need you right now."

Okay, maybe he *was* going to win this argument, but it wasn't done yet. When J'avet dismissed the room, I jumped up from my seat and stalked over to him.

"I'm coming too," I said firmly.

He barely glanced at me. "No, you're not. The decision is made and is final. You can cry on Brinley's shoulder, then continue on to Agus like you're supposed to. Or better yet," he looked at me directly now, "go back to Earth where you belong."

"Fuck you," I spat.

"That attitude is precisely why you're not ready for missions like this," he said calmly. "I need clear heads, not emotional ones."

"I can be clear and calm," I told him, being calm. *See, asshole?*

"Only when you're reminded," he said. He crossed his arms over his chest and glowered. "You would be nothing but a liability and a distraction."

I narrowed my eyes at him. "Is that what this is about? My relationship with Slek and Zarex?"

"And Danec," he said cooly. "They will all need to focus. They can't do that with you there."

I gaped, then pressed my mouth in a line. "You don't have much faith in their professionalism."

"I have utmost faith that, when not distracted, they'll do their jobs," J'avet said.

I hesitated for a moment. "This isn't about them, is it? It's because *you* find me distracting."

The way his eyes flicked away gave me all the answer I needed.

"You want me to stay behind because you're finding it hard to keep it behind your pubic plate.

Yeah, Slek told me all about that. Good way to hide your reaction to someone else. Someone like me."

"You're way off," he snapped. "Even if you weren't, it's irrelevant. Orders are orders and yours are to stay here."

"You're not my commanding officer," I pointed out.

"I'm captain of the *Chimera*, that's all the rank I need to keep you off my ship. Now say your good-byes. We leave within the hour." Before I could say another word, he turned and stalked out of the room.

I hid my tears until Slek put his arms around me and drew me to his chest.

"It's not forever," he said softly. "Just while we deal with the Iri and get Danec back. As soon as that's over, we'll meet on Agus. All four of us. Um, five with Brinley. She's kind of one of us."

"Yes, she is," I sniffed. She was definitely part of the family, odd little family though it was.

"You two will have each other. You won't have to share the chocolate," he said, his tone light.

I snorted. "I'd rather have you guys around and never have chocolate again."

Wait, was I crazy? No, it was just…love

I leaned my head back and looked him in the

eyes. "I love you."

He kissed me lightly on the mouth. "I love you too. Can you believe it? The biggest player in the IF, settling down."

I gave him a lopsided smile. I wasn't sure if he really was a player or just talked the talk. I knew he hadn't glanced at another woman since we met, apart from flirting with Kalvix.

"How about that," I agreed. "I guess I better help you both to pack."

"It shouldn't take long." Zarex placed a hand firmly on my ass. "I have an idea for something we can do to pass the time after that."

"Funny, I had the same idea," Slek said, a sly smile on his face.

It took me a moment to realise exactly what they proposed. When they did, I blushed.

"Both of you? At the same time?"

"I'm game," Slek said.

"I'm reasonably certain there's nothing he can give you sexually that I can't," Zarex said, a swagger in his tone. "But I'm game too."

"You can't give her three cocks all by yourself," Slek pointed out.

Zarex opened his mouth, closed it, then nodded. "That's true. Between us, we'll have that covered."

I didn't know what to say or think, because between them, I was about to melt into a puddle on the floor.

"Maybe we should start, um, packing, before we run out of time," I said around a dry throat.

"*Chimera* won't leave without us," Slek said.

"It's J'avet, anything is possible." I took his arm and Zarex on the other and we left the briefing room and headed to Zarex's. It was closer and bigger and Slek's was always a mess.

Zarex opened the door and waved us both inside.

The door barely closed behind us when they both descended on me in the best way possible. Clothes went flying this way and that. I think they all had their seams intact, but I would make no guarantees about that. Right now, I didn't care. I was naked before I could blink more than once or twice.

These guys meant business. Good, so did I.

I don't know how we moved from the door to the bed, but the next thing I knew, we lay next to each other, Zarex's tongue teasing the insides of my thighs, while I licked the tip of Slek's cock.

Hells yeah.

I opened my mouth to take him in deeper and sucked. Zarex licked my folds more firmly.

"Awww yeah." Slek wound his fingers through my

hair and held me while he thrust in as deep as I could take him. Several times he hit the back of my throat and groaned.

I would have smiled if I didn't have a mouthful of dick. Not having a gag reflex for the win.

I was so occupied with running my tongue over his tip and tasting his juices, that I almost missed my own orgasm. Yeah, I know, right? It went through me so hard and fast, I hadn't seen it coming. Pun intended.

Slek pulled out of my mouth to let me breathe, and scooted down until we were face to face. He kissed me while Zarex slipped one of his cocks into me from behind.

I groaned against Slek's mouth.

He chuckled and drew back a little. "Just out of curiosity…"

I thought he was talking to me, until I saw him look right past me.

I glanced over my shoulder and saw Zarex smile.

"Can I be inside two at once?" Zarex asked. "I can, if they're close enough together. And…into that sort of thing."

"I've always thought you were pretty hot," Slek said with a lopsided smile, which was also sideways from where I lay. "And smart."

I didn't even raise my eyebrows. Slek's comments about Danec's ass, and other things, already suggested his interest lay with men as well as women.

"Well then." Zarex manoeuvred us until my pussy was as close to Slek's rear as possible. "Lucky I can expand a bit too."

I stared over my shoulder as his cock seemed to grow longer, almost as long as my arm.

"I'm officially jealous and aroused," Slek declared.

Zarex smiled. The cock he'd slid into me, all wet with my juices and his natural lubricant, he slid carefully into Slek. The other, he slid deep into me.

Oh. My. Gods.

With a pleased smile on his face, Zarex began to thrust.

Slek groaned. At first I thought it was in discomfort, but I soon realised it was in pleasure.

I slung my arm over him and gripped his cock with my hand. With every one of Zarex's thrusts, I worked my hand up and down.

"Hells yeah," Slek groaned.

Zarex grunted. "This doesn't seem fair." He slid out of me and rolled me so I lay in front of Slek and he was behind.

"That works too," Slek muttered. As Zarex thrust

into him, he slipped his cock into me.

After a moment of trying to work out the rhythm, we managed to move in unison, thrusts and bucks, thrusts and bucks. Sweat and moans of pleasure.

The nodules on Slek's cock rubbed my insides into almost absolute delirium. I lifted my leg to let Slek in deeper and glanced over my shoulder. Seeing Zarex pounding into Slek while Slek pounded into me was hands down the hottest thing ever. The only thing missing was Danec. I slipped a finger into my mouth and pretended I was sucking on him.

That made me come again, harder than I ever had before. So hard I probably drenched Slek, but he was busy coming himself. Zarex wasn't far behind. He fit his orgasm between Slek's first and second.

"Coming twice," Zarex panted. "Now *I'm* jealous."

I laughed, but it took me a long time to come down. Partly because I was floating somewhere outside the ship, and partly because I didn't want to. I closed my eyes and enjoyed the feeling of being with two amazing guys. The three of us and Danec would be together again, whatever it took. I would make sure of that. Maybe if J'avet would lighten up…

I pushed him out of my mind, determined to appreciate the moment, and the guys, while it lasted.

EPILOGUE

I stood at the window beside the pod bay and stared out at the stars. The galaxy looked empty. No sign of the *Chimera*. I had hugged both guys and kissed them soundly in front of J'avet, because fuck him.

I held in tears while they waved goodbye and stepped into their pod. I choked back a sob as the door slid shut, blocking my view of their faces. I curled my hands into fists at the metallic clunk of the space doors opening.

The first tear trickled down my cheek when the pod slid out the door, toward the *Chimera*.

Brinley put an arm around me and we watched the pod become smaller and smaller.

I was almost sure I saw Slek wave and I waved back vigorously. Who knew if he saw me or not.

The tears fell freely when the pod disappeared into the *Chimera's* pod bay. The door closing, shutting them in, seemed painfully final.

"We'll see them again before we know it," Brinley said. "A week. Maybe two."

I nodded, but I wasn't sure she was right. It might be months. It might be years. It might not be at all. I had no way of knowing what they were heading into. The Iritauri might shoot them on sight. They might...

I wiped my eyes and watched the *Chimera* move away.

I watched until she was nothing but speck.

Then she was gone and my guys with her.

***

WILL Edie see her guys again? Will J'avet stop being an asshole? The story continues in Star Protectors.

ABOUT THE AUTHOR

Maggie Alabaster writes reverse harem and, paranormal, sci-fi and fantasy romance.

She lives in NSW, Australia with one spouse, two daughters, one dog, and countless birds.

Sign up for my newsletter! Sign Up!

Join my reader group! Join here!

Follow me on Bookbub! Click here to follow me!

Check out my website- www.maggiealabaster.com

Dark Masque

Book 1 Bait

Book 2 Prey

Book 3 Trap

Saving Abbie

Book 1 Pitch

Book 2 Pound

Book 3 Session

Book 4 Muse

Book 5 Rhythm

Book 6 Encore

Novella Venomous

Ruthless Claws

Book 1 Ivory

Book 2 Crimson

Book 3 Elodie

Harmony's Magic

Complete collection

Short reads

Taken by the Snowmen

Jingle All the Way

Also by Maggie Alabaster and Erin Yoshikawa

Caught by the Tide

Book 1–Pursued by Shadows

Book 2 Pursued by Darkness

Book 3 Pursued by Monsters